MW01257746

"If you're
I'm comin

"Agreed." Miriam just needed a few minutes alone to regain control of herself.

She was almost to the barn when a hand grabbed her and whirled her around.

She found herself face-to-face with Devon McCallister, one of the cousins who'd helped Owen escape. And he was a killer, just like Owen.

"The cops are here," she said, her voice louder than normal, hoping one of them would hear her.

Devon sneered. "I saw 'em pull in. That young cop and his girlfriend don't scare me. I have a car parked on the next road. They'll never find me."

Before he could say anything more, she wrenched her hand free and shoved the heel of her hand against his nose. Blood spurted, splattering her pristine dress and the front of his shirt. He cursed, both hands going to his broken nose.

She whirled around and took off running toward Caleb. "Caleb!"

A gunshot barked behind her. The bullet brushed her skirt and hit the ground in front of her.

She might not survive the next one...

Dana R. Lynn grew up in Illinois. She met her husband at a wedding and told her parents she'd met the man she was going to marry. Nineteen months later, they were married. Today, they live in rural Pennsylvania with their three children and a variety of animals. In addition to writing, she works as a teacher for the deaf and hard of hearing, and is active in her church.

Books by Dana R. Lynn

Love Inspired Suspense

Amish Country Justice

Visit the Author Profile page at LoveInspired.com for more titles.

HUNTING THE AMISH WITNESS

DANA R. LYNN

LOVE INSPIRED SUSPENSE
INSPIRATIONAL ROMANCE

LOVE INSPIRED® SUSPENSE
INSPIRATIONAL ROMANCE

ISBN-13: 978-1-335-95716-0

Hunting the Amish Witness

Recycling programs
for this product may
not exist in your area.

Love Inspired
22 Adelaide St. West, 41st Floor
Toronto, Ontario M5H 4E3, Canada
www.LoveInspired.com

Printed in Lithuania

MIX
Paper | Supporting
responsible forestry
FSC® C021394

If we confess our sins, he is faithful and just to forgive our sins, and to cleanse us from all unrighteousness.
—*1 John* 1:9

To my son Bradley and my daughter-in-law, Hannah (8-17-24). I pray that your marriage is filled with blessings and joy.

ONE

Miriam Troyer gently set the baby carrier she'd lugged up the stairs to her second-floor apartment onto the floor. Her blond braid flopped over her shoulder, thanks to the rain pounding the thirsty June grass outside. If she'd taken the time to look at the forecast before she'd accepted a new client's last-minute plea to clean his house prior to an impromptu retirement party, Miriam could have retrieved her daughter from day care and gotten home long before the downpour began. At least the canopy on the car seat had protected the baby from the weather. Ella Mae, her precious nine-month-old daughter, was teething again and would be cranky until her two top front teeth, which were pulsing beneath her gumline, pushed their way through.

Which meant when Ella Mae was asleep, Miriam took every precaution not to disturb her. Still, she could not resist the urge to brush the tiny girl's silky blond curls back from her forehead. She never knew she had the capacity to love deeply until Ella Mae entered her life. All her previous selfish dreams and worries had been crushed by the overwhelming emotion her daughter inspired.

Unlike her late husband.

Her lip curled. They'd lived from paycheck to paycheck since the day they'd married. When they were suddenly in the green with no explanation, suspicions bloomed in her mind. He hadn't received a promotion at his day job. Nor had he, to her knowledge, taken up a second job. He hadn't ever been one to be glued to his cell phone, yet suddenly he was constantly texting and leaving the room to accept phone calls. Also, even though he'd previously turned off his phone at nine o'clock every night, he began taking calls at all hours.

Then he started leaving the apartment on weak excuses.

When she overheard a conversation that sounded like a drug deal, that was her line in the sand.

Miriam hadn't been a saint growing up, but she refused to raise her unborn child with a drug dealer. Secretly, she'd begun to make plans to leave him. It would be difficult. Making her own way while being pregnant created complications. Who wanted to hire a pregnant woman?

That brought a new concern. She could not remain in their town. Once news of Tim's illegal doings became known, and Miriam had no doubt they would, she and their child would be tarnished by his bad reputation. She'd felt enough shame in her life. She didn't need any more.

She shoved his memory from her mind and dug around in the backpack slung over her right shoulder. The bag doubled as her purse and a diaper bag. Locating the keys, she reached out to unlock the front door. The moment she touched the door, though, it swung inward about four inches, then stopped.

What? Dina, her roommate, should have left by now. She worked the afternoon-and-dinner shift at the local bistro. It was close to four in the afternoon. The hair on the back of Miriam's neck stood on end. Dina's work ethic was well known. She'd never call in sick to work unless she could not leave her bed. And the bistro didn't have enough servers.

They'd never tell Dina not to come in. If anything, they'd beg her to take two shifts in a row. And she'd do it to save up for her next semester at college.

Something was wrong.

Miriam shoved the door. It would not budge, as if something heavy was leaning against it.

A second later, a blood-streaked hand flopped to the ground in the opening of the door. Horror swept through her. Although she couldn't see the body attached to the hand, there was no mistaking Dina's drugstore press-on nails and the gold bracelet on her wrist, a gift from her boyfriend last Christmas.

She was dead.

For a moment, Miriam froze. Memories of a different night nearly a year ago hijacked her brain. Five days before she'd planned to leave her spouse while he was out of town on a "business trip," she'd woken to shouts and a loud bang, and had rushed to the kitchen as fast as possible even though she was entering the third trimester of her pregnancy. She arrived in time to see Tim, her husband of eighteen months, sliding down the wall, leaving a smear of blood on the otherwise pristine primrose-yellow paint.

A noise shook her from the nightmare raging within her. She jerked up her head. A man with dark eyes and a scruffy beard stared back at her. He held a gun in his hand.

She knew those eyes. She'd seen them the day Tim had been killed. She'd worked with the police to get his image out so he could be captured. In fact, he'd been caught and sentenced to life in prison. But he never made it to the high-security prison. She'd been informed his cohorts had broken him out on the way to the prison, killing three guards in the process.

It had been Miriam's description that had been responsible for his capture and his sentence. The moment she learned of his escape, she'd known he'd come for her, and had moved to a new location, hoping to blend in and live with her daughter in peace. Everyone had known her by her married name, Miriam Barnes. She'd legally changed both her and her daughter's names back to Troyer in a bid to remain hidden.

She'd worried about where he had disappeared to. And now, he stared at her, hatred in his gaze, a malevolent snarl on his lips.

Her husband's murderer had escaped justice and tracked her down. He raised the gun.

Grabbing the doorknob, she slammed the door shut. A thump hit it. Dina's body must have fallen against it. She ducked to grab the baby carrier a millisecond before a bullet smashed through the wooden entrance. Exactly where she'd been standing.

She'd grieve for Dina later. Right now, she and Ella Mae were in mortal danger. Hefting the carrier in one arm, she dashed to the steps and fled back the way she'd come. The car seat banged against her thigh. She'd have bruises for sure.

Ella Mae squawked.

Please, baby. Go back to sleep. Just until we get to the car.

Her silent plea went unanswered. The baby wailed, kicking her legs in anger. Miriam tightened her grip on the carrier and rushed toward her small four-door sedan. It was hard to see the vehicle through the heavy rain, but she always parked in the same spot. She clicked the door locks and ran the remaining length of the lot. Her feet pounded through puddle after puddle, splashing cold water on her blue jeans past her knees. The casual sneakers she wore to clean houses squished, completely drenched.

Her car loomed in front of her. Arriving at the vehicle, she snapped the carrier into the base located on the back seat behind the driver's seat and slammed the back door. She opened her own and threw herself behind the wheel. At the abrupt movement, her cell phone fell from her pocket and clattered to the wet cement. The apartment-building door crashed open. Jerking her car door shut, she abandoned the phone. She'd barely made it as it was. She hit the brake pedal and pressed the start button. Her fingers trembled. If she still had a key start, she never would have been able to do it. The engine roared to life and she backed up, her tires squealing. She nearly careened into the killer. He leaped out of the way just before her bumper would have crunched into his legs.

Wrenching the gearshift into Drive, she stomped on the gas. Her window shattered. A bullet struck her upper arm. She cried out. The burning pain nearly overwhelmed her. Only the sound of Ella Mae shrieking in the back seat kept her grounded in the moment.

She swerved out of the lot and into the late-afternoon traffic, cutting off another car. A horn blared behind her.

She thought she'd be safe so close to Columbus, Ohio. Although she wasn't in the city, the area surrounding her apartment had a robust population. She had begun to feel secure. Using her maiden name gave her a false sense of anonymity.

Help. She needed to call for help. She glanced at her dashboard display. *No phone connected.* Her stomach quivered. Her phone was lying in the parking lot at the apartment. She could drive to the local police department. She'd made sure she knew where it was when she'd moved.

Sweat broke out on her forehead. She'd lost him before. Could she make it from her car to the interior of the building without him shooting her, or injuring her daughter? Not if she had to take the time to unhook the car seat.

Ella Mae had stopped crying and was hiccupping behind her.

No, she could not risk her baby. She'd accept death herself if it would protect her child, the one person in her life she'd ever loved without selfishness or ulterior motives. Nothing mattered except keeping her little girl safe.

She glanced at the row of cars behind her in the rearview mirror. Which one belonged to the killer? The red light turned green and the cars began to move through the intersection. She might make it through before the light turned again.

A green truck raced along the right shoulder, clipping her side mirror.

Miriam's blood froze. She needed to move. She could not wait for her turn.

Swerving into the left-turn lane, she cut off another car. He hit the horn. She could see the driver shouting at her. Probably nothing pleasant, either.

"Sorry, buddy. Better you get cut off than become collateral damage if he starts to shoot."

Holding the steering wheel with both hands, she spun her car as fast as she dared. The car waiting at the light had pulled too far into the intersection. Miriam's left bumper nudged it. She absorbed the jolt without slowing down. If she hadn't feared for her life, she would never have fled the scene of an accident, even such a tiny one. However, her priorities had gone through a major shift in the past fifteen minutes.

Zooming past the police department, she hoped an on-duty officer would see her speeding and give chase. But then, he'd be in danger, too. Terror had begun to confuse her thoughts. It didn't matter. No police cars came after her.

She risked another glance in her rearview mirror. The green truck bore down on her. Miriam's stomach plummeted. She would not make it.

Pressing her lips together, she stomped her foot on the gas pedal until it rested on the floorboard. She kept to the left lane. The traffic in front of her melted away, the drivers shifting into the right lane when they saw her coming. Her fingers clutched the steering wheel like vise grips, and her knuckles ached. Miriam had grown up in an Amish community. Although she'd left to experience the thrills and adventure of the *Englisch* world, driving fast had never been one of them. She tended to get motion sickness in a car. The familiar roiling built inside her gut. It could have been fear or the movement, or a combination of the two.

She glanced back. The green truck wasn't behind her anymore. In relief, she allowed herself to slow down. But she didn't stop. Briefly, she considered heading back into town and stopping at the police station. No. She had to keep going. Just because she didn't see the truck, didn't mean he'd stopped tracking her.

Owen McCallister had tracked her down once. He wasn't going to stop just because she'd outrun him. She knew in her soul he was still back there. And he'd keep coming for her.

An hour later, she drove past a large white sign with red block letters on the side of the road.

Welcome to Sutter Springs, Ohio. Come Visit Our Amish Community!

Sutter Springs. Home. Or it had been. In her ignorant

youth, she'd sneered at all those who flocked to the town, a burgeoning tourist attraction outside of Berlin County. Why were they so interested in Amish culture? She'd grown up Amish and had chafed at all the restrictions. She could not cut her hair. Could not use technology. Could not go to high school with some of the *Englisch* girls she had befriended. Nor could she date outside of the community or have an exciting job.

And the worst, in her mind, was she was supposed to marry a man her *daed* approved of, have a bunch of kids, and spend her entire life tending a house instead of enjoying a fulfilling career.

She snorted. She'd left the community and the experience had been a sour, shameful one.

Except for Ella Mae.

If only she could go back. But *Daed* was dead. He'd been gone for nearly four years. Her baby sister, Beth, had married Gideon Bender, Miriam's former beau, and they were starting their own family. She'd started to reach out to Beth. Had made plans to return. Then she'd gotten cold feet. She hadn't even attended Beth's wedding. Six months later, she'd met and married Tim Barnes after a whirlwind courtship, only to learn her husband wasn't who she thought he was.

Her car stuttered to a stop. She glanced down at the dashboard. She'd run out of gas.

For a moment, she sat, astonished. Wait. What was she doing? She had to move!

Miriam pushed open the door and scrambled out of the car. She needed to get as far from the vehicle as possible, quickly. She opened the back door and slipped her arms through the straps on the backpack, then pulled the car seat out of the car. Should she leave it?

No. If she needed to put Ella Mae down, she didn't want to set her on the wet ground. Plus, the capsule added a layer of protection. Hopefully, an unnecessary layer.

Although the seat bumped against her thigh when she pulled it from the vehicle, the baby had gone back to sleep, lulled by the movement of the car. Thank goodness.

She walked along the side of the road. Her feet squelched in the soggy sneakers. Every few steps, they were sucked into the soft mud lining the road. Once, she nearly lost a sneaker when she yanked her foot back.

Exhausted and defeated, she peered around her. A small farmhouse loomed in the distance with an Amish buggy in the driveway. Several cows and a horse grazed in the pasture. If only she knew whether there was a business phone in the barn. She could go to them and plead for assistance.

Sutter Springs was a town where the *Englisch* and Amish lived and worked side by side, while still holding true to the *Ordnung*.

An engine roared behind her. Her hands grew clammy. She tightened her grip on the car-seat handle so it wouldn't slip out of her grasp. She knew without looking that Owen McCallister had found her again. A hasty glance over her shoulder confirmed her suspicion. Hefting the car seat closer, she ran, tears streaming down her cheeks. She had no chance of outrunning him.

She and Ella Mae were going to die.

Maybe she could save Ella Mae. He was after her. Not her daughter.

She felt the heat of the truck on her back. Running as close to the grass as she could, she bent long enough to slide the car seat down the incline of the grass, then kept running. She only made it ten steps before the truck hit her, sending her flying. Spinning in the air, her eyes couldn't track the changing scenery.

As she crashed to the ground, pain lanced through her head, then Miriam lost consciousness.

Caleb Schultz replaced his screwdriver into its slot on his tool belt and stood back to survey his work. Everything looked wonderful. The new cabinets he'd installed were a definite improvement from the previous ones, which had sustained serious damage after a kitchen fire. Satisfied, he gathered the rest of his supplies and hurried through the back door of his client's *haus*, intending to pack up his buggy before the rain returned and drive home in time for dinner. He placed the tools in a box in the back of the buggy, keeping the netting in place so it would not shift around too much while he drove. The netting was his own invention. Sometimes his *mamm* and younger sister rode in the buggy while he was between jobs. The net allowed him to store his tools without risking injury to the two women he cared for.

He sighed. Someday, Rhoda would married and leave home, and then it would be just he and his mother.

That would be a sad day for him. Although, he knew it was the way the world worked. Even among his friends, he and Lucas were the only ones not married, although since Lucas's wife died, he didn't count. Caleb didn't think he'd ever get married. For one thing, his *mamm* needed him too much. She was feisty, but her wheelchair restricted what she could do alone.

Once, he'd planned on getting married. Just a few years ago. But the young woman he'd courted had died from meningitis. After that, he shoved aside all thoughts of romance. He had a family to care for and a cabinet-making business to pay the bills.

It was enough.

He closed the back of the buggy and took three steps towards the *haus*. He needed to let Lucas know the cabinets had been installed. Oh, wait. He needed to give him the final invoice.

Pivoting on his heel, Caleb started back to his buggy.

He halted when movement on the road caught his attention. A woman was walking along the side of the road, carrying one of those modern baby car seats the *Englisch* were so fond of. Even from the distance, he could tell she was distraught.

His mouth dropped open in disbelief as the woman sent the car seat down a wet, grassy slope on his client's property. Seconds later, a green pickup truck rammed into her, flinging her body into the air. She flopped like a broken rag doll. The truck shifted gear and fled, the tires squealing on the wet pavement.

Caleb blinked, more shocked than he'd ever been. He ran up the porch stairs and opened the back door. He stuck his head inside and bellowed.

"Lucas!"

Lucas Beiler rushed from the *haus*. "Caleb? What's wrong?"

"I'll explain in a moment. *Cumme!*"

Without waiting to see if his friend followed, Caleb ran down the steps, the heels of his work boots clopping like horse hooves on the wooden planks. He didn't head toward his buggy but thrust himself into the field. The grass was already knee-high. He forced his way through it. Between the resistance of the grass and the way his boots sank into the soggy earth, it was nearly as bad as trying to run on sand. He didn't stop.

He heard the *boppli* crying. Screaming, actually. The car seat had landed upside down, the hard arc of the handle pressed into the ground, keeping the child from landing face down and possibly getting smothered. The poor *kind* had to be terrified.

"Shhh. It's *gut*. Don't cry, little one." Gently, he upended the seat. A little girl, around the same size as his ten-month-old niece, Gretta, blinked up at him, tears dotting her round cheeks. Her lower lip stuck out. Those deep blue eyes were pools of anxiety. Blond curls covered her head.

Lucas crashed to a halt beside him, puffing loudly. "Who would abandon a sweet *boppli* here?"

"She wasn't abandoned." Caleb narrowed his eyes and scanned the field. "There."

He pointed at the body lying on her right side twenty feet away. "I'm going to check on her mother. Someone ran into her."

Leaving the *kind* with Lucas, Caleb hurried to the mother. Was she alive? He could see blood on her left arm through her thin gray cardigan. Her dark denim jeans were wet and stained with mud, although he didn't see any blood on them. As he reached her, she moaned.

He froze in place. His knees weakened. She was alive. Still, her eyes remained closed. A rock near the right side of her head had streaks of blood on it. When he edged around to that side, he saw a red trickle.

Dropping to his knees, Caleb pulled off his light coat and wadded it into a ball. He pressed it against her wound. She moaned again, then let out a soft whimper.

"Sorry. I don't mean to hurt you. I want to stop the bleeding."

When she didn't respond, he removed his gaze from her wound so he could check the state of her arm. That bleeding seemed to have stopped. He returned his perusal. His gaze snagged on her face.

She was familiar. He wasn't sure how, but he knew he'd met this woman before. Had she been a nurse in the hospital? Caleb had been in coma for three years after a drunk driver had smashed into a community Amish picnic he'd attended with his family. He'd come out of the coma six years ago to find his father had died at the picnic, his *mamm*'s legs and spine had been damaged, and his next younger sister, Molly, had sustained injuries that left her with a permanent limp. Molly and two of his other sisters had married since. He, *Mamm* and Rhoda had lived with Molly and her husband for a year until Caleb bought a small *haus* for the three of them, so Molly and Zeke could have more room to raise their growing family.

He shook his head. She wasn't one of the nurses he recalled seeing at the hospital. He was sure of it.

"What do we do?" Lucas asked, setting down the car seat on the ground between them.

That's when he saw the backpack lying on the ground behind her, both straps broken. "Bring me that bag."

Lucas lumbered over and snatched the backpack. Caleb stretched out his hands. The heavy weight of the bag pulled his body forward. After setting it beside him, he glanced inside and found several plastic bottles filled with water and a can of *boppli* formula, as well as a container of cereal and several changes of clothes. He also found a wallet. "We can at least feed and change the *boppli*." He frowned. "There's no phone to call for help."

Lucas rubbed his bearded chin. Even though he was a widower, once married, an Amish man always wore a beard.

"I thought *Englischers* always had their phones on them."

Caleb shrugged and peered around them. The lush green grass contrasted with the dark rolling clouds above them. Lucas followed his gaze and straightened.

"I'll go get the buggy. We can get her inside my *haus* and warm her up, then I will take the buggy and go to the community phone to call a doctor."

Caleb nodded. "I'll wait with them."

He watched his friend disappear back through the grass. A squeaky noise made him turn back. The little girl began to fuss, shoving her tiny fist into her mouth as if she could eat it.

"Are you hungry, little one? I think I can take care of that."

Caleb grabbed the can of formula he'd spotted and read the instructions twice. He opened the formula, then measured some out and put it into a bottle. Next, he shook it to mix the liquid and powder. When he moved it close to the *boppli*'s mouth, the fierce little one clung to it with and opened her mouth wide, giving him a brief view of two tiny teeth on her lower gums before she began to noisily drink the formula.

He nearly shut the backpack but stopped when he saw the wallet. If the woman had a driver's license, he could find out who she was. Maybe even find a way to contact her family. He lifted it from the bag, then flipped it open, ignoring the cash. He wondered at the lack of credit cards. From what he knew of the *Englisch*, they always carried them. He focused on the driver's-license picture staring up at him from behind the clear plastic. The feeling of familiarity struck him. Then he looked at the name and his mouth dropped open.

Miriam Troyer. He'd known a Miriam Troyer years ago. As *kinder*, they'd lived in the same district. Then the number of families had expanded so much that the district had separated into two. He hadn't seen her in years. Although, he'd heard she'd left the Amish for the glitz and glamour of the *Englisch* world.

Miriam Troyer wasn't an uncommon name among the Amish. It was possible this Miriam wasn't his former acquaintance.

He glanced at her face again. Her blue eyes were open. He knew those eyes. They roamed his face, her brow furrowed. Pain and confusion mingled in her eyes.

"Miriam! You're awake. How do you feel?"

She didn't answer. Her frown deepened. Finally she spoke. "Sir, do I know you?"

He couldn't blame her for not remembering him. He hadn't recalled her name at first. "It's *gut*. I'm Caleb. Caleb Schultz. We used to be in the same district."

Then he remembered about her father. He should offer his condolences, even though it was several years too late. "I am wonderful sorry about your *daed*, Miriam."

Those blue eyes widened. Her already pale cheeks turned ashen. "I don't know who you are." Her lips trembled. "I don't know what you're talking about."

"Miriam…"

"And I don't know if my name is Miriam!"

A chill settled in his heart. She had amnesia. She was the only one who might have been able to identify the hit-and-run driver. Was it an accident, or had it been a case of road rage?

Or even something more sinister?

Caleb recalled the drunk driver that had plowed into

the picnic years ago. Since his brush with the dark side of human nature, he had developed a cynical streak.

Still, only Miriam could tell what really happened. But not until she remembered her own identity.

TWO

Caleb peered down at the woman on the ground, his mind whirling with this new and unexpected twist. He hadn't seen Miriam in years. Not since they were both teenagers. Even though Miriam had left the community, Molly would have let him know if she'd returned. After all, Molly's brother-in-law, Gideon, was married to Miriam's sister, Beth.

Beth, as far as he knew, hadn't heard from her sister in years. She'd certainly never mentioned a *boppli*.

Did she even know that her father had died several years before? Amos Troyer had died a violent death. Caleb had been there when he'd been put to rest.

Miriam hadn't shown up. People had talked about it. Not in front of Beth, of course, but gossip happened everywhere. Beth had always been well liked. Though Miriam had been able to charm people when she was growing up, by the time she'd left, many had said good riddance.

How would she feel now, learning about all she'd missed?

He shuddered, recalling awakening from his coma to learn his own *daed* was gone. That knowledge had devastated him. In an instant, he'd gone from being a teenager to the man of the *haus*, and dealing with three younger, grieving sisters.

Molly helped. Of course, she did. But she was already starting her own family by the time he had regained consciousness.

And his poor *mamm*. The driver had run over her, breaking her legs and her spine. She'd lost the use of her legs that awful day. Now, she used a wheelchair wherever she went and suffered from chronic pain. But she never complained.

Caleb sighed. He'd have to tell Miriam if she could not remember. He wasn't looking forward to that conversation. But she needed to know. Hiding the truth never helped anyone.

How was he supposed to fill in the blanks of her life for her when she could not even recall her own name?

A sudden cry broke his attention. Shifting his gaze to the other victim, the little one was kicking her legs, leaving him no doubt as to what she wanted. He leaned in close. *Ella Mae* was stitched neatly across her blanket.

He recalled sitting with Miriam when they were still in school. They'd been talking about their favorite books. She'd said hers was about twin sisters named Ella and Mae. The sisters were brave and virtuous. They went on many adventures and always championed the weak and downtrodden. But she liked them for all the wrong reasons. She liked Ella and Mae because they were both blond and beautiful, and everyone admired them for their physical attributes and not because of what they'd done or what they stood for. One of the *maidels* in school had seen the pictures on the covers and had told Miriam they looked like her. Had the teacher known she was reading those books, she surely would have confiscated them and burned them. They had done nothing but fueled Miriam's vanity and her wish for admiration.

Had she ever learned the true value of the Ella and Mae

characters, or was Miriam still the shallow, selfish *maidel* he'd known so long ago?

He pushed away the thought. It didn't matter. He had a duty to help. At least he now knew their names, even if he knew nothing else.

He'd help, and then as soon as possible, he would send them on their way.

"*Ack.* Poor *boppli.* She wants to be freed from this contraption you had her in."

Miriam's pain-glazed eyes flared wide. She jerked her head, then groaned. "Ow."

"Don't move too much, Miriam. You hit your head hard on a rock. It hurts wonderful bad, *ja?*"

Her lips smashed together and her brow furrowed. "It does."

Ella Mae continued to squirm. If he didn't do something soon, she'd start screaming and carrying on. He could not say he blamed her. The way she was strapped in would make him cranky, too. Although, he had to admit, the carrier had likely saved her life.

Smiling at the little one, he unhooked the bands holding her down, then lifted her out. When he tucked her close, she snuggled for a moment before turning and reaching for Miriam with a whine.

"Your *mamm* isn't feeling well, Ella Mae. Let me hold you for a minute, *ja?*" He swayed, trying to soothe the *boppli* with motion. It usually worked with Gretta. Ella Mae settled against him, but her pretty blue gaze remained fastened on Miriam.

"*Mamm?* I'm a mother?" Panic coated each word. "How could I be a mother? What kind of person am I that I forgot my own child?"

He had no idea how to respond to her query. The woman

before him now, even though it was the same Miriam he'd once known, had changed. He could not tell her anything about her life, or her *kind*. Or, he thought, frowning, her husband. He glanced at her left hand. She wasn't wearing a ring. Did that mean anything? Miriam had always been selfish and strong-willed. Had she changed since she left?

Lucas arrived with the buggy, stopping about eight feet from the small group on the ground. Caleb approved. No sense getting close enough that anyone could be kicked by a hoof if the gentle mare spooked.

Lucas climbed off the buggy. "It looks like rain again."

Caleb squinted at the sky. The clouds had darkened and roamed the sky in thick clusters. The breeze had a definite nip in it. "*Ja.* Let's get Miriam and Ella Mae back to your *haus*."

Lucas didn't question the names Caleb threw out at him, but he also didn't know Miriam had lost all her memories. Miriam glanced at Lucas with apprehension. He couldn't blame her. She had to be terrified and off-balance. "Miriam, this is Lucas, a friend. We're going to his *haus*."

She slowly nodded.

"Can you stand if I help you?" he asked her, passing Ella Mae to Lucas.

She attempted to rise on her own power. When she swayed, he rushed to her side and assisted her. She cried out when her left arm bounced off him.

"Careful. You hurt your arm somehow. And I don't know if you broke anything when the truck hit you."

She paused. "I was hit by a truck? While I was in a car?"

She glanced around, probably searching for the vehicle and wondering why they were in a field and not in the car.

He shook his head. "*Nee.* I saw it. Someone hit you while you were walking. You must have known you were in danger, though, because you slid Ella Mae down the slope a few seconds before he hit you."

Why she hadn't slid down the slope as well, he could not say. He imagined she'd panicked seeing the vehicle looming behind her.

Lucas made an impatient motion. "*Cumme.* We can talk later."

A couple of raindrops plopped on Caleb's head to prove Lucas's concern. Miriam hadn't stabilized on her feet yet. If they didn't want to get soaked, they'd have to hurry.

"I am going to carry you to the buggy," he informed her.

Her mouth dropped open and her pale cheeks flushed. "I don't think…"

A low rumble of thunder rolled above them.

"Okay. Fine."

He lifted her as carefully as possible, making sure her right shoulder was against his and not the injured left one. The last thing he wanted to do was injure her more. Although he didn't typically carry fully grown people, he sometimes had to carry his wheelchair-bound mother. Plus, he was a carpenter. He lifted heavy loads of wood and tools every day of his life except Sunday. Carrying Miriam Troyer wasn't going to be too much to handle.

"This is so awkward," she muttered.

When he glanced down, her eyes were glued to the horizon. Hmm. He'd never thought of Miriam as being modest or easily embarrassed. Could a lost memory change someone's personality?

There were so many questions in his mind.

They made it to the buggy. He placed Miriam on the bench in the back. Lucas had gone back and retrieved the baby carrier and the backpack, but little Ella Mae wanted nothing to do with the contraption. When Lucas attempted to lower her into it, she stiffened and screamed.

Caleb shook his head. In such proximity, the holler made his ears ring. He wouldn't have been surprised if the neighbors down the road heard her. "That's the loudest *boppli* I ever heard."

"Ja!" Lucas agreed. "And I can't get her back in."

"Give her to me," Miriam commanded.

That was more like the Miriam he remembered.

Caleb watched as the woman enfolded the *kind* in her arms. She looked awkward and scared, but there was also a naturalness to the way she held the little one. She might not remember being a mother, but her instincts hadn't abandoned her just because she'd forgotten.

She was a mother.

How could she forget such a thing? Looking down at the baby laughing in her arms, Miriam swallowed. Emotion clogged her throat.

The buggy swayed and jolted. Lucas drove them back toward the house. It was awkward, she thought again. Maybe she knew these men. But she didn't know if she did. She had seen the one who carried her look at her ring finger. She'd glanced at it, too, and had been a little alarmed to see that she wasn't wearing a wedding ring. If she was a mother, shouldn't she be married? She wasn't dressed the same as the gentleman, so she assumed she wasn't Amish.

Then why did the one man seemed to know her?

She had so many questions. Her body ached. And her stomach churned. When the child in her arms wiggled closer and nestled her head against Miriam's shoulder, warmth spread through her. Not warmth from the baby's body heat. It was inside her.

She didn't remember this little girl. But she knew that the man was correct. She was her mother. How had they come to be here? And where was their home? Too many questions whirled in her head. She could not prioritize.

When she shifted, her entire right side and her left shoulder protested. It was like she had a horrendous rug burn over her entire body. Casting her glance down, she grimaced. Her jeans had so much grass and mud on them, she wasn't sure what color they were supposed to be.

Why would someone hit her and drive away?

"We're here."

Startled, she jerked her head up and looked into the man's eyes.

"Who are you?" she breathed.

"Sorry." He flushed. "I'm Caleb. Caleb Schultz. I introduced myself earlier, but I s'pose you had a lot on your mind. Let's get out of the rain. I'll explain everything inside. I promise."

She nodded. She would not get any answers sitting in the buggy by herself. Lucas approached and held out his arms for Ella Mae. The baby, thankfully, allowed herself to be handed over. Miriam definitely didn't want to deal with the screaming again.

Caleb assisted her into the house, then helped her to a soft couch in the front room, insisting she stretch out her legs. "Lucas covered it with a spare blanket when he came back for the buggy. You can be comfortable here while we call for a doctor to *cumme*."

She wanted to argue. It made her feel vulnerable to recline like this, covered with what had to be a handcrafted quilt. How she knew that she could not say, only that she knew she could recognize hand-sewn versus machine sewn.

Ella Mae started to whimper and fuss.

"I think her teeth hurt." How she knew this, she wasn't sure. When Caleb dug around in her bag and pulled out a small tube of gel for soothing a baby's tender gums, she blinked. Somehow, she hadn't pegged him as a man that knew much about children. He handed it to her. She opened it and squeezed out a dab on her finger. She swiped the gel along her baby's sore gums. Instantly, the child settled down. When Ella Mae yawned and rubbed at her eyes, he used a damp towel to clean her face and handed her over to Miriam. Within moments, Ella Mae's thumb went into her mouth and she closed her eyes. Miriam kissed the soft curls on top of her daughter's head and melted back onto the armrest of the couch.

She really needed some pain meds. Sighing, she turned her attention to Caleb. Talking to him might distract her from the aches and pains raging all over her body.

"Okay. Now that Ella Mae is sleeping, how do I know you?"

He hesitated.

"Was it that bad?"

"Bad? *Nee.* It's been many years since I knew you. Your family used to be in the same district as mine when we were *kinder.* Then our district split and we didn't see each other regularly anymore."

"Wait. I was Amish?" Suddenly, it made sense why the culture seemed so familiar.

"*Ja.* But like I said, it was a long time ago. I heard you left the community, oh, several years back. Close to ten years ago, I expect. I haven't seen you since."

She frowned. "You said I was walking. Why?"

He shrugged. "I don't know. I saw you get hit and I ran to get to you. I didn't realize who you were until I saw you."

"Were we friends?"

The pause was longer this time. He ducked his head. "I take it we weren't."

"We were *kinder*."

An evasion if ever she heard one. And he still would not meet her eyes. There was something he didn't want to say. Which made her all the more determined to hear it. Having her mind filled with fog rather than memories made her flesh crawl. She needed any memories he could give her to fill the void. Even unpleasant ones. Anything would be better than the vast nothingness inside her head.

The sound of a car pulling into the driveway cut their conversation short, and they both looked at the open doorway. Lucas led an older man into the room. The doctor pushed his glasses up his nose with his finger and peered at Miriam. "I hear you've had some excitement this afternoon."

"Yes. Please. Can you look at my daughter first?"

"Absolutely." Ella Mae's examination only took a couple of minutes. "She seems to be teething. You might want to pick up something for that."

"I will."

"Good. Now, let's have a look at you."

Caleb stood and approached the other men. "She has a couple of obvious injuries. Also, she has lost her memory."

Lucas's jaw dropped. The smile disappeared from the doctor's face. When he began his examination, Lucas motioned for Caleb to join him in the hallway. Miriam was torn. She wanted privacy. At the same time, Caleb was the only person she knew of who knew her at all. But before she could think of a reason for him to remain, Caleb picked up Ella Mae and followed his friend from the room.

She answered the doctor's questions as well as she could, but until she'd awakened to find Caleb hovering over her in that damp field, everything was blank. The doctor probed her injured head. Miriam winced, even though he was taking care not to cause her additional pain.

He moved on to the wound in her arm.

"Lucas!"

She startled at the doctor's sudden yell. Lucas and Caleb both stampeded into the room.

"I want you to tell me about the hit-and-run driver again."

"I didn't see anything," Lucas said.

Caleb described what he'd seen. "I thought it was cold-hearted for the person to leave the scene of an accident."

The doctor turned a stern eye on all of them. "It was no accident."

Miriam gasped. "What? Are you saying he deliberately hit me?"

"I am. I'm also telling you that he was out to kill you. That arm didn't get hurt when you were hit. That's a gunshot wound."

Her mouth fell open. The bottom of her stomach dropped. Thinking she'd been hit accidentally by some coward who could not face what he'd done had been bad. Knowing someone had tried to hurt her on purpose was much worse.

THREE

"Someone shot me?" Miriam blurted. "Why?"

She looked at the doctor, then at Caleb and Lucas, as if one of them might have the answer. Caleb and Lucas shook their heads.

"That's what we need to find out." The doctor pushed his glasses up his nose, sighing. He gathered his notes together and closed his bag. "I'll need to report this to the police. It's normal procedure whenever there's this kind of wound. I imagine they'll want to interview you."

"But I don't know anything." Miriam clasped her hands together to keep them from shaking.

"Still, they'll want to talk to you. It's possible that when they talk with you and try to go through what happened, you might remember something. Don't try and force it, though. The memory is a funny thing."

She nodded, still stunned by what she'd learned. She was also appalled that someone would come after her, knowing they'd be coming for an infant as well. Her stomach turned. Why would anyone hurt her sweet baby girl?

"On a positive note, despite being hit by a truck, you don't have any broken bones. I've taped your ribs. They're bruised, but there's not much more I can do for you than that. Your head will ache for a few more days. You knocked it pretty good. I think you might have a slight concussion, so I'd like to get you to come into the hospital to run some tests. You should limit your screen time. Do you have a phone?"

Did she? She lifted her eyebrows at Caleb.

He shook his head. "I didn't see a phone when we found her. We had to check her bag for identification. Maybe we missed it."

"Well, if you did and you find a phone, try to avoid it, Miriam. Those screens can bother your eyes and head, even when you haven't got an injury. In addition, your muscles may be sore, so take it easy for a few days. But it seems you were close enough to the edge that he more or less pushed you over, rather than hit you."

The doctor shoved to his feet and headed to the door. "I'll make the report to the police. I can give you a lift to the hospital. I will—"

"No!" Fear crawled up her throat. Her head swung around as she looked for her daughter. She didn't remember the child, but knew she loved her all the same. Every instinct warned her against separating from her child. There was no way she'd meekly go along with such plans. Her gaze landed on Ella Mae, safe in Caleb's arms. Safe for the moment. She meant to do all she could to keep her that way. "I can't go to the hospital. What about Ella Mae? I won't leave her. She's all I have."

What if someone decided that since she had no memory, she wasn't fit to be a parent. Could she lose her daughter?

The doctor's brow scrunched. Out of concern or puzzlement, she could not tell. Nor did she care. Could he force her to go if she didn't want to? "Are you declining care?"

The way her head pounded told her that would not be the best choice, either. "Can't I come into your office during normal business hours? So I can keep Ella Mae with me? I'm afraid someone will take her from me since I have no memory."

"I doubt that."

She would not be moved.

Another worry crept into her mind. Did she have insurance? What if she didn't? And she didn't know what she'd do tonight. She hadn't seen any women yet. But Lucas had a beard. So he was married. Although she wasn't as comfortable with him as she was with Caleb. But Caleb didn't have a beard. She could not stay with a single man in his house, alone. It would not look right.

She held in a snort. Someone had tried to kill her—twice, according to the doctor—and she was worried about her reputation in a house where no one except Caleb knew her.

The doctor scratched the back of his neck. "Well, I can't force you to go to the hospital. I would like to get an X-ray on your ribs. Just to be on the safe side. But I think you'll be okay for a night. Tell you what. Tomorrow is Thursday, so I'll be in surgery in the morning. I will be back in the office at ten or somewhere around there. Come in then. I will put you on high priority when you arrive, so either myself or my partner will fit you into the schedule."

"I'll get her there," Caleb assured the doctor.

"See that you do. In the meantime, this young lady needs some rest this evening."

"I will make sure she does."

Miriam raised her eyebrows at him. She wasn't sure if she resented his presumption or appreciated the support. Probably a bit of both. She had the feeling she wasn't used to relying on others. It made her wonder once again if she had anyone out in the *Englisch* world on her side. If only she could remember.

"Hey."

She glanced up to find Caleb standing next to the couch. The doctor and Lucas had both left the room. She'd been so focused on her internal thoughts that she never noticed them leaving. Ella Mae was asleep in her car seat.

Caleb squatted so they were at eye level. "You look worried."

"Well, yeah. I have no memory. And someone wants me dead. I'm not sure why. And I don't know where I will stay even for the evening."

Caleb pursed his lips. "You can stay here."

"Will Lucas's wife mind?" She would not be surprised. Asking a woman to house a strange woman and her child would be a burden.

Sorrow crossed his features. "Joanna died two years ago."

She sighed. She wasn't the only one with problems. "Poor Lucas."

Caleb stood and thought for a moment. "I'll take you with me. Maybe one of my sisters has room. It's only for the night. Once tomorrow comes, we can get you checked out and then find a way to get you home. Your address is on your driver's license. It won't be hard to find it."

Alarm bells went off in her head at his words. She swung her legs over the edge of the couch. "I can't go home."

She didn't know how she knew it. She had no memories of her home. Wherever that was. But she knew if she went back there, she'd end up dead. No. If she wanted to protect her daughter and save her own life, she needed to hide.

If he could not help her, then she'd have to find the strength to do it on her own.

Caleb sprang forward when Miriam moved, closing the gap between them when she lurched to her feet. His arms shot out and steadied her when she staggered. Once he was certain she could stand without falling over, he released her and gave her space, staying close enough to catch her if she lost her balance again.

His cheeks warmed. When she'd first awakened, he hadn't thought anything of holding her. She needed his help. For the first time, he realized he'd taken a stranger into his arms.

He shook the notion from his head. There was nothing inappropriate about his actions. The truth was, though, Caleb was nearing thirty-four and had never held a woman he wasn't related to before. It unnerved him, how pleasant it felt.

Such ideas weren't productive. He needed to find out why she was so insistent she could not go home.

"Miriam. What do you mean, you can't go home? Have you remembered something?" If she could remember anything, it would be wonderful *gut*. Any memory would help.

She shook her head and wrapped her arms around her waist, hugging herself. "No. I still can't remember. I just know I can't go home. Especially since I don't know who is after me or why. What if he comes after me again? He'll know me, but I won't know him until it's too late."

"Let me think for a moment."

She had a point. Even though he'd seen the truck, neither he nor Miriam could give a description of who was after her. And he didn't know much about *Englisch* vehicles. He certainly could not identify the make and model of the truck that had hit her. They pretty much looked the same to him. All he'd be able to tell the police was that the vehicle was green. That wasn't much information. It probably would not be helpful. There had to be hundreds of green trucks in Ohio.

He sighed. As much as he was glad he'd seen her and could help, there was a definite downside. Even as a *kind*, Miriam had been intense. Hanging out with her could be exhausting at times because it always meant there'd be drama. She tended to get bored easily.

Growing up, it had meant arguments or challenges to see who could do what. Now, apparently, the drama had escalated into risking one's life. What had she gotten herself into?

Caleb didn't want to get too invested in Miriam's life. She was a beautiful woman with an adorable daughter. But she was also a woman who'd once scorned and flaunted the rules he lived by and broken at least one heart in the process. And he didn't want to bring her trouble into his own home.

Shame twisted inside him. How could he deny her assistance because she was in danger? When he was in a coma, someone had targeted Molly. If Zeke Bender hadn't stepped in to help her, Molly and his mother, and maybe even his other sisters, Rhoda, Betty, and Abigail, might have died.

"Let's find you a place to stay tonight, *ja*? We can figure out the rest in the morning, ain't so? My sister Molly has an interesting family. One of her brothers-in-law is a US Marshal. Another used to be a bounty hunter."

She blinked at him. "An Amish woman is related to a bounty hunter."

He tucked in the edges of his lips to prevent his smile from popping onto his face. He didn't want her to think he was laughing at her. "*Ja*. A former bounty hunter. And her sister-in-law is married to a police sergeant. We can talk with one of them."

She didn't look convinced, but he had seen the spark of intrigue in her expression. His gut unclenched. She would not flee in a panic. The Miriam he'd known years ago would have hightailed it out of there the moment she knew trouble was coming.

Except it was trouble that had brought her in the first place.

"Caleb. *Cumme*." Lucas motioned to him from the doorway. "Dr. Spade has a flat tire. He needs help changing it."

Caleb smiled at Miriam and excused himself. He stepped out into the cool afternoon and made his way over to the doctor's SUV. The rear driver-side tire was a pancake. A large, crooked nail protruded from it.

"I wonder when you ran over that." He gestured to the nail.

"It could have been anywhere." The doctor grimaced. "The way it's wedged in there, I might have had a slow leak for a day or two. Maybe jostled it to make it worse."

"*Ack*. We'll change it. Maybe you can save the tire and have someone repair it. You have a jack and a spare?"

"Do you think they can do that?"

He shrugged, amused that he, an Amish man who lived in a community that didn't allow rubber tires, seemed to know more about tires than the *Englischer*. Lucas didn't bother to hide his own chuckle. A second later, Dr. Spade laughed, shaking his head.

"I know. Don't think I can't see the irony in needing your help with this."

Laughing a little, the three men started to change the tire. Fifteen minutes later, Caleb stood at the open tailgate and wiped his dusty hands on a towel Lucas handed him while Dr. Spade threw the ruined tire into the back.

"That should do it," the older man announced.

A movement out of the corner of his eye caught his attention. He frowned as he watched a man in the distance walking along the side of the road. He'd seen more strangers walking along the road today than usual. Gazing farther up the road, a single vehicle was parked along the shoulder.

A truck, the same color as the one he'd seen knock Miriam over the edge.

"I think we should go inside."

Both of the men followed his gaze.

"Caleb, isn't that a green truck? Like the one you saw earlier, say?"

He nodded at Lucas. "*Ja*, it looks the same."

As a group, they headed back to go into the *haus*. Dr. Spade had his cell phone out. "I'll contact the police."

They took three more steps.

The first bullet caught Dr. Spade. He toppled over, dragging Caleb with him. The second bullet hit Lucas. Caleb shifted under the doctor's weight in time to see his friend fall. The green truck roared past the *haus*, spitting dust in its wake.

All possibility that Miriam had nearly been run over by accident fled from him. Someone tried to kill her. She was being hunted.

Miriam's killer hadn't given up on his prey.

FOUR

What had Miriam brought into their peaceful Amish community?

Caleb eased the doctor off him, holding him to avoid bumping him around and hurting him further. When the older man groaned, Caleb winced.

"Sorry, Doctor. I don't mean to hurt you."

"Don't worry about me. Look—look at Lucas." Harsh gasps punctuated the doctor's breaths.

Caleb crawled over to Lucas. His friend's eyes were open, but they had a glazed look that Caleb didn't like at all. Perspiration dotted his forehead, but it wasn't that hot out today. The damp ground beneath him could not be comfortable, yet neither man complained of the wetness seeping into their clothes.

This was bad.

"What do I do?" he spluttered.

"Here." A feminine hand pushed a folded towel toward him. His head whipped up.

Tears streaked Miriam's pale face, but her expression had hardened into a determined mask. She stepped to the doctor, holding her injured arm close to her body. A second towel was lying across her shoulder. "We have to try to stem the bleeding. Press that to his shoulder. Don't unfold it."

He placed the towel on Lucas's wound.

"No. Not like that. You have to apply pressure. Otherwise he'll keep bleeding."

"Do what…she says." The doctor coughed. "Don't stop."

He pressed the folded cloth to the wound as instructed. Lucas gasped.

Miriam moved past them to the other injured man. She kneeled next to the doctor, looked him over, and frowned. "Where was he shot?"

"My back." The doctor's complexion had become gray. "The ground is putting…pressure on it."

"What do we do now?" Caleb hissed at Miriam, feeling helpless. "Lucas doesn't have a phone in his barn. I don't want to leave you, Ella Mae, and my friends here alone. What if your hit-and-run driver returns?"

For a moment, he considered getting in the doctor's car, but Caleb wasn't sure he could drive it. Nor did he trust Miriam, with her scattered memory, to recall all the traffic rules and the ins and outs of driving a stick shift.

Miriam thought for a moment. "The cell phone!"

She scrambled to her feet and ran a few steps to where the doctor's cell phone sat on the ground. Caleb had forgotten the older man had been holding it when he was shot.

"Passcode…" The doctor rattled off a number. Caleb wasn't sure what he meant. He'd never used a cell phone before, not even in his work, although the bishop allowed them for some businesses. Miriam, however, seemed to understand. She tapped some buttons on the keypad.

A moment later, she set the phone on the ground beside Caleb.

"Nine-one-one. What is the nature of your emergency?" a slightly monotone voice asked.

"I need help. Someone shot two of my friends." What other information should he give him?

The man on the other end of the line continued. "Are you safe?"

"For now. The man who shot at them drove away."

"We're sending an ambulance and the police to your location." He rattled off Lucas's address. "Is that where you are?"

"*Ja!* We are in front of the *haus*."

"Remain on the line. If the shooter returns, go inside and lock the doors."

"Should we try to bring the injured men inside the house?" Miriam yelled.

"If you can do so safely."

"I can stand," Lucas mumbled. He pushed himself off the ground and wobbled. Caleb lunged to his feet and caught his friend before he fell to the ground again.

"I'll help you." He glanced over his shoulder. "Miriam, can you *cumme* with us? You can stay inside with Lucas while I help the doctor."

She firmed her lips but didn't protest. Her concerned glance toward the man still on the ground informed him she was worried about the older man. So was he. But he'd worry less if she was not sitting out in the open.

They made it into the front living area before Lucas's legs gave out. Caleb all but dragged his friend to the couch. Lucas had lost consciousness. "Remain here," he told Miriam. "I hope the ambulance will be here soon. I'm going to go get Doctor Spade."

She nodded. He didn't wait to see more but bolted out the door. He paused a moment on the steps and looked around. Seeing no other cars or trucks, or strange men with guns, he ran the rest of the way and dropped to the doctor's side.

Had anyone helped his father while he lay dying after the drunk driver smashed into him? Caleb remembered little of that day. They'd only been at the picnic an hour before disaster had struck, leaving tragedy and pain in its wake.

Now, Miriam had brought disaster again. Why had *Gott* allowed this? And why had she *cumme* to Sutter Springs? He recalled the selfish *maidel* she'd been growing up. Had she grown out of that, or had her self-centeredness caused this?

"Doctor Spade, we need to move you inside."

The doctor's lids fluttered, and he grimaced. "No use."

"No use? I don't understand." Fear clenched his gut. He hoped he didn't understand.

The older man opened his eyes. They blinked and fastened on Caleb with awful finality. "I won't make it."

He shook his head. "*Nee.* The ambulance—"

"Won't matter." The doctor coughed. Blood flecked his pale lips. Caleb fought to keep his countenance calm. "My lungs…filling with blood. So weak."

Caleb wanted to scream against the unfairness. Dr. Spade had *cumme* to help, on his own time. Because he was a *gut* man, a man who enjoyed helping others. He would pay for that generosity with his life.

Miriam stepped out onto the porch. The hot anger bubbling in the pit of his stomach rose, along with the distinct flavor of bile. He shot a glare at her. None of this would have happened if she hadn't returned to Sutter Springs and interfered with his life. He knew he wasn't being fair, and that she had been at risk herself.

Still, the rage at the suffering before him needed an outlet, and she was there.

Miriam paled and halted. She whipped around, then fumbled for the doorknob and staggered into the dark *haus*, disappearing from his view. Guilt tore at him. But he ignored it and turned back to the doctor on the cold, wet ground.

Sirens pierced the gloomy grayness. They'd be too late.

"Caleb…" Dr. Spade's voice wobbled, a slight wispy sound. He clutched weakly at the younger man's arm. "Caleb, listen to me."

Caleb swallowed. He could not speak, so he nodded. When he looked at his doctor friend, he imagined he saw his *daed*.

"Always protect the innocent, my boy."

As if the words had drained him, the man closed his eyes with a long, drawn-out sigh. Caleb didn't need to check his pulse to know Dr. Spade was dead.

The ambulance drove up the gravel driveway and stopped in front of the *haus*. They were too late for Dr. Spade, but maybe they could still help Lucas.

He still had 911 on the phone, he recalled. "The ambulance is here."

"You may end the call, sir."

He hung up and waited. When the ambulance crew approached, he stood and backed away. Of the two men approaching, he recognized the older paramedic, Blaine. During a barn raising last spring, two boys fell off a roof and the paramedics came out. Blaine had been among them. His somber gaze met Caleb's. A gunshot wound was never something to be taken lightly.

His eyes switched to the other paramedic. He was younger and a stranger to him. Probably a new hire. He still had that eagerness about him. As if he hadn't been on the difficult calls yet. Ones where someone died.

That was about to change.

Blaine addressed him. "Hi, Caleb. I heard the police will arrive in a minute."

Caleb nodded, knowing all the emergency units shift to the same radio channel once a call has been acknowledged.

The younger man approached with jaunty steps. He faltered when he saw the body on the ground.

"It's Doctor Spade!"

"I see that, Sam." Blaine kneeled beside the doctor and felt for a pulse. Five seconds passed. Shaking his head, he sighed and rose to his feet. Then he looked at the shocked white face of his colleague. "Call it in, please."

Sam's voice trembled when he requested a coroner. Caleb flinched at the words—*dead on the scene*.

He didn't want to watch them cover the doctor's face and load him into the coroner's vehicle. They needed to see to Lucas, anyway. "Lucas Beiler, the other injured man, is inside. He was bleeding wonderful bad."

"You go, Sam. I'll wait for the coroner."

Sam nodded and followed Caleb.

Miriam cradled Ella Mae in her good arm and moved out of the way when the young paramedic rushed into the house like someone was after him. Her stomach clenched as she took in his pale and haunted face. It was never good when those coming to provide help looked like that.

She hung back out of the way while the paramedic tended to Lucas. She avoided Caleb's gaze and made sure to keep the width of the room between them. He didn't need to use words to tell her he blamed her for Lucas and the doctor's injuries. His glare had done that, just fine.

Was he wrong? Had she somehow brought the killer to them? Without her memory, she could not answer her own questions. All she knew was that she and Caleb had known each other long ago. Apparently, what he had known about her then hadn't encouraged him to think well of her now. She had no defense. What if she was a horrible person?

Ella Mae fussed, gnawing on her fist. Hadn't she eaten just an hour ago? She must be going through a growth spurt. Miriam ducked her head so she would not have to meet Caleb's accusing gaze and went to her backpack. Now what? She only had one good arm to work with, and it was already busy with her daughter.

"Here. Give her to me."

She hadn't heard him approach. She wanted to ignore him, to handle the situation on her own, but Ella Mae would be the one to suffer from her belligerence. Instead, she handed her daughter to the Amish stranger and sought out a bottle and baby food. She kept her head down so their eyes would not meet.

She'd seen the anger and accusation when he'd come in. She didn't need to see it again.

She also could not stay here. Because of her, two good men were injured.

The paramedic working with Lucas stepped into the hall. "I have him stabilized enough to travel."

"Gut."

Miriam reached for Ella Mae. Caleb handed the baby back to her without a word.

The door opened. A police officer entered with the older paramedic. "Caleb," said the paramedic, "this is Sergeant Yates. He needs to take a statement from you."

"Ja, I understand."

The paramedic looked at her. With a quieter, gentle voice, he said, "Ma'am? He'll also need to talk with you."

"That's fine."

"Good."

"This guy's ready to roll, Blaine." The young paramedic's voice was calm, despite his wrecked appearance.

"Good work, Sam. The coroner arrived. He's taking care of Doctor Spade."

"Coroner?" Her world shrunk. Their voices were coming through a tunnel. Then her ears buzzed…

Miriam came back, lying on the sofa in the front room. Three men stood around her, hovering. Heat seared her face. The two paramedics and the police officer straightened when they saw her eyes were open.

She noticed Caleb wasn't one of the concerned men standing around her.

"I'm okay." She started to sit up. Three pairs of hands shot out to assist her. She waved them away. "Seriously, guys, I'm fine."

Suddenly she recalled the baby had been in her arms before she fainted.

"Where's Ella Mae?" Her eyes darted around the room.

"I have her." Her gaze landed on Caleb. He stood a few feet away. "When you fainted, I grabbed her. She's not hurt."

"Oh! Thank You, God!" she whispered fervently, meaning the prayer with all her heart.

Ella Mae patted her face and gave an anxious cry. She gnawed at her tiny fist, making growling noises, reminding Miriam of a puppy.

"I think she's still hungry."

Amazed that he was speaking to her, she gave him a quick smile. "Yes. She's a growing girl." The other men weren't paying attention to her. She cast him a shuttered glance. "Kinda surprised you're talking to me."

To her amazement, his face flushed all the way to his ears. "You can take her into the kitchen and feed her there.

Lucas has a high chair his sister uses when she and her children visit him."

Apparently, he wasn't going to respond to her comment. It had been a bit snarky. Without opening her mouth again, afraid she'd say something that would offend him and make him revert to the man with the angry glare, she scooped her daughter close and headed to the next room.

The paramedics took Lucas to the ambulance. She heard him speaking to Caleb. That was a relief. If he was conscious, it was a good sign, wasn't it?

Sergeant Yates followed her into the kitchen. When she went to get the high chair, he motioned her aside and grabbed the chair for her. "I don't want you hurting that arm more. Where do you want this?"

She pointed to the table. "Set it at the end of the table. I'll sit next to it."

He nodded and followed her instructions. "Do you need me to put her in the chair?"

"I can handle that."

He stood back and didn't speak or interfere as she carried her daughter over and buckled her in.

Ella Mae banged her small fists against the plastic tray.

"All right, sweet girl. Give Mama a moment. I need to clean this tray before you eat."

She gathered what she needed, and cleaned the tray and her daughter's hands efficiently, if a little awkwardly, with one hand. After the uncertainty of not knowing who she was, knowing what to do to take care of her child eased some of the tension pulling at her shoulder blades. But it was as if they were connected to rubber bands someone was stretching to the limit.

She dragged the chair closer to the baby and sat. Ella Mae hummed when offered a bite of cereal. She opened her mouth wide. She wasn't content to wait for Miriam to bring the spoon to her. Her entire head darted forward like a turtle to capture the utensil in her mouth.

Miriam laughed, covering her mouth to keep the sound from disturbing anyone. And by anyone, she meant Caleb.

Why did she care what he thought? It's not like she knew him. What had he said? They used to belong to the same district. According to him, it had been some time since she'd left the Amish, but she still understood their culture. When a community grew too large for one bishop, which was about nineteen or twenty families, it divided and another bishop was appointed to handle the second district.

How could she remember all that, but not her own child, or her parents? She froze.

Did she have family in the community? Sisters or brothers? Was her mother still alive? Her grandparents?

The peace she'd felt feeding her daughter dissipated as new questions about her life came at her like a barrage, attacking her mind.

"Miss, are you all right?"

Startled from her dark thoughts, she jerked back in her chair. The sergeant stood in front of her.

"Sorry?"

"You looked a little scared."

Scared. Angry. Lonely. Overwhelmed. Pick an emotion. Any or all of them would work for her current mood.

But, of course, she would not tell him that. "I'm fine. Sergeant—"

What was his name again?

"Yates. Sergeant Yates. I need to ask you a few questions."

She waved at the chair across from her. She had a feeling this would be a frustrating conversation for both of them.

He sat down and started with easy enough questions. "Your name is Miriam Troyer."

She nodded. "That's what my driver's license says."

"Where do you live?"

"Hold on. Watch her." She scrambled off her chair and ran to the other room to find her wallet. She dug it out as she walked back to the kitchen. "Here it is."

She handed him her driver's license.

"You really don't recall anything about yourself?"

She shook her head. "Sometimes I'll do something and it feels familiar, like feeding Ella Mae. But I have no idea what I can or can't do until then."

He leaned back in his chair and stared at her, his eyes narrowed to mere slits. "Let's try this. Tell me about your accident."

"It wasn't an accident. According to the doctor…" She paused to take a deep breath, trying to tamp down her sense of guilt. "According to him, I was shot. Being shot and nearly run over is too much for me to believe it was an accident."

"Don't forget the fact that he came back for you."

She whirled around in her chair. Caleb stood framed in front of the window, his face in shadows. His voice had been neutral, however, when he moved closer, she saw his features clearer. The anger was still visible, except it wasn't directed at her anymore.

He met her gaze. "I'm not mad at you, Miriam. Someone tried to kill you and Ella Mae. They did kill Doctor Spade and hurt Lucas wonderful bad. Even if you had angered someone in Columbus, which I could see happening, you didn't deserve to die. Neither did the others."

"Why do you say you could see her irritating someone?"

He faced Sergeant Yates. "I knew Miriam years ago."

"She might have changed."

Why were they talking about her like she wasn't here? Talk about irritating someone.

"*Ja.* Maybe so. Or maybe not. The Miriam I knew as a kid was a stubborn flirt who wanted things her way and didn't care who she hurt as long as she got what she wanted."

Horrified, Miriam listened to him categorize her various faults. She could not still be that way, could she? A flirt? Was she that selfish?

Seeing herself through his eyes, she didn't like the picture emerging.

FIVE

Sergeant Yates stood. "I don't know if it will help, but I do think you should come into the police station and look through our database. See if anything jogs your memory."

Caleb leaned his shoulder against the doorframe, his arms crossed. Now that Miriam knew his true opinion of her, or rather, of who she was, she had no other option than to find her and Ella Mae a place to stay instead of relying on the kindness of strangers.

Even if the strangers knew her.

She grabbed her wallet and her driver's license. Before putting them back in her bag, she surreptitiously looked inside. She had some money shoved into the pocket of her wallet. She dug around inside her bag. There was a small pocket on the back. After unzipping it, she found a single credit card and a debit card. She must have been paranoid about something to keep them there and not inside her wallet. Did she dare use them? She had no idea if she had any money in the bank account or if she had a balance on the card.

Her teeth worried her lower lip. If she left, could the man set on killing her find her if she used the cards? Or was that something only law enforcement could do? Maybe since she was in danger, the police would pay for a hotel room?

She didn't want to ask in front of Caleb. That would give him one more reason to disdain her, she was sure. However, she would gladly suffer through his disdain if it meant protecting Ella Mae.

The little girl was becoming crankier. She needed to move around. Miriam cleaned her up and released her from her high chair.

"I need to change her an let her play for a few minutes. She's getting restless."

"I'll be on my way. Will you bring her by the station tomorrow?" the sergeant asked Caleb.

She responded instead. "I was thinking about that. Would not it be better if you dropped me off at a hotel?"

Both men swiveled around to stare at her. The sergeant's expression held a polite smile. She focused on that. Caleb's blank face unnerved her.

"You would not prefer to remain with your friends?"

She scoffed. "I don't remember them. And you heard his description of me. Does that sound like he wants me hanging around him?"

Sergeant Yates's eyebrows rose to his hairline. "You have a point. Let me call in to my chief and see if we can make this work," he said and went off to make the call.

She nodded, then began the work of repairing the mess Ella Mae had made of her hands, her face, and the high chair.

"Ella Bean, what have you done to yourself?"

"Ella Bean?" Caleb asked. "Is Bean her last name? The blanket only said Ella Mae."

She frowned. "I don't know if it's her name or a nickname. It just kind of slipped out."

Maybe she had something in her bag with her daughter's full name.

"I showed Sergeant Yates my driver's license. I'm sure with that information, he can find everything he needs to know about me. I would not be surprised if he already has it. There's a strong possibility that when he returns from talking to his chief, he'll know more about me than you do."

If her voice sounded a little snarky, she wasn't about to apologize. She'd had enough. It's not like she intended to cause him trouble. Since she hadn't seen him in years, and obviously they weren't close even then, she highly doubted she'd come this way to see him.

After removing her now reasonably clean daughter from the high chair, Miriam carried her into the other room. She settled her on the sofa, penning in Ella Mae with her own body, and dug around in the backpack for a clean diaper and wipes. Her mind continued working furiously as she changed her daughter then found a few toys in the bag. She took the throw off the back of the sofa, then spread it on the floor and set down Ella Mae down with the toys.

Ella Mae giggled and grabbed at the plastic toys.

By this time, Miriam had worked herself into a fine state of righteous anger. How dare he judge her like that. Caleb had no clue what she'd gone through. Well, neither did she, but it must have been bad. She'd been on foot and had been shot before being mowed down by a man in a truck who liked to shoot people.

Her conscience twinged at that thought.

She still didn't see how any of it was her fault. Just cleaning up Ella Mae made her injured arm hurt, although she'd been careful to use her other arm, mostly.

The immensity of her problems overwhelmed her. She fought the urge to throw herself on the sofa and have a hard cry. It would do no good, and it would be difficult to watch her daughter if she was busy having her own meltdown.

Such behavior would only cement Caleb's supposition that she was a diva.

Granted, he hadn't said those specific words, but she understood what he'd meant.

"I'm sorry for what I said," a gruff voice said behind her.

Miriam stiffened her shoulders. She didn't want to face him. Not until her eyes were free of the tears. She blinked them back and slowly rotated until they were face-to-face.

His own eyes narrowed as they zeroed in on hers. "I made you cry."

She hadn't hidden her reaction as well as she'd hoped.

She shrugged off his words as if they were unimportant. "It's not you. It's this whole situation. And I didn't cry. Not yet. Maybe once Ella Mae goes to bed I can, but I don't have the time for that nonsense right now."

His mouth dropped open at that statement.

She'd surprised him. He probably expected her to take every opportunity to grab the spotlight. But that wasn't her. She was no longer the girl he'd once known.

Too bad he'd not have the chance to learn that about her.

Sergeant Yates banged through the door, startling Ella Mae. When she began to cry and crawl toward her, Miriam dropped down on the floor and sat cross-legged. She pulled the child onto her lap to soothe her, wincing when her injured arm protested.

"Sorry." The police sergeant ducked his head at her. "Didn't mean to startle the kid."

"She's fine. No worries."

Caleb cleared his throat. "You called your chief? Did you learn anything?"

The sergeant nodded. "A car was found on the road a little way back. It was registered to Miriam. It had run out of gas."

She frowned. "So that explains why I was on foot."

"I should also tell you that there were three bullet holes in the car doors. A window had been shot out."

She gasped.

He wasn't done.

"And the tires had all been slashed. After you'd left the car, of course."

She sat on the floor, blinking, holding her child in her lap, unable to process what he was telling her.

"What about the hotel she asked about?"

Huh. He was probably anxious for her to be gone and out of his life.

"A little hang-up there. This is the Sutter Springs Annual Amish Festival."

Caleb groaned.

"What?" She looked back and forth between them. "The Amish are having a festival?" That didn't sound right.

Caleb took pity on her and explained. "The town of Sutter Springs is a growing tourist attraction. Every year, the town puts on this festival, inviting *Englischers* to *cumme* and explore our way of life. Some families host dinners and cooking demonstrations, there are tours at businesses and buggy rides. Most of the businesses hold sales or auctions. They do those throughout the year, but this week, there will be a lot of attractions."

She glanced at the sergeant. "Which means?"

"The hotels and the local bed-and-breakfasts are booked. They have guests on waiting lists. I can take you to the station and we can see what we can find…" He shrugged.

What was she supposed to do now?

"She can *cumme* and stay with my family."

Caleb regretted the words the minute they left his mouth.

Miriam's blue eyes flared wide, shock in their depths. After his rant in the kitchen, she thought he hated her. He hadn't been welcoming.

Shame burned in his soul. His *mamm* would be wonderful disappointed in her *sohn*. She'd raised him better.

Sergeant Yates nodded as if the problem was solved. Miriam didn't agree. She shook her head with such force her blond hair swirled around her shoulders.

"Uh-uh. I can't stay with you. I'd only be bringing more trouble to your doorstep. Look what happened to Lucas. And that was minutes after I arrived."

He had to admit, it impressed him that she wasn't complaining about what he said. Instead, she was talking about him being in danger. While his opinion of her rose slightly, his own embarrassment in himself grew in proportion.

"I know I've been a bit impatient—" he ignored her when she muttered "grouchy" under her breath "—but it was what happened. It wasn't directed at you personally."

The stare she leveled at him told him quite clearly she didn't believe him. He could not blame her.

He glanced at Ella Mae, who was snuggled in her arms. As he watched, her eyelids drifted closed. "You can't bring the *kind* into a police station. If you *cumme* home with me, my *mamm* and my sister Rhoda will be on hand to help with her. Your arm and head can rest, and I can take you to the police station tomorrow and you'll be able to leave her at home."

She pressed her lips together and looked away from him.

"I'm going to go out on a limb here and say I think Caleb's plan makes sense," Sergeant Yates said. "We don't have anywhere for you to stay where you'll be comfortable with a baby. And your arm complicates matters. What if you can't do something you need to do to care for her?"

Fear crossed her face. He recalled her conversation with the doctor.

"Miriam." He waited until he had her attention again. "No one is going to take Ella Mae from you. You are her mother, and from what I've seen, you're a wonderful *gut* one."

"But my memory loss—"

"Has not impacted your ability to care for her." He never would have expected that from the Miriam he'd once known. How much had she changed? Once again, his awful words rang in his mind. If he could, he would erase them.

She scanned the room. "I can't stay here. It's Lucas's house. It would not be right."

"The man in the green truck knows you are here," Caleb added.

She paled but nodded. "That's true. I guess I should be grateful Sergeant Yates's police car is sitting in the driveway. That may keep him away for the time being."

"It may," Caleb agreed. He wanted to push but held back. Having four sisters had taught him to wait and let them make up their own minds.

"And I can't stay at a hotel." She sighed. "I guess I'll take you up on your offer."

She didn't sound pleased about it, but at least she'd said yes.

"How do we know my attacker won't follow us to your house?"

Sergeant Yates took that one. "We'll load you into his buggy from the back door. You'll have to keep down, of course. I'm figuring that between an Amish buggy and a police car, he'll assume you went with the police car."

Her head popped up. "What about the ambulance?"

"He may think you went with them—"

She shook her head. "I mean, will the drivers be safe? If he thinks I'm in the ambulance, will he attack it?"

Caleb's heart pulsed in his ears. Was his old friend still in danger? He'd known Lucas most of his life.

"The ambulance and the coroner both left while we were in the kitchen. I'm sure my radio would have gone off if the ambulance hadn't arrived. The driver would have let the hospital know they were on the way, so the emergency room would be prepared for their arrival."

Little by little, they were negating her arguments.

Ella Mae squirmed and made bubbly noises in her sleep. He grinned. She was an adorable *kind*. Miriam's gaze settled on him. When he looked her way, she regarded him, her mouth twisted in thought. That was an expression he remembered. She wore it when she tried to solve a puzzle of some kind.

He could not be sure, but her anger toward him seemed to have softened while he watched her daughter. "Are you sure your mother and sister won't mind the inconvenience?"

"They won't mind. *Mamm* and Rhoda both enjoy taking care of others. They'll think it a special treat, having you stay with us."

Miriam had always been able to charm the adults. Of course, the rumor that she left the community for an *Englischer* had circulated years back, but maybe it'd died down. Even if she remembered or knew of Miriam's past, his *mamm* wouldn't say anything. No one outdid Esther Schultz in graciousness.

He grinned.

"What has you so happy?"

He laughed. "My *mamm* will be overjoyed to have Ella Mae in the *haus*. She loves *bopplin*."

She sat for a few seconds longer, then straightened her posture. "Well, I guess I'm going to your house. Can one of you take Ella Mae so I can stand up? It will take me just a minute to pack up her stuff."

SIX

To Miriam's surprise, Caleb didn't hesitate to bend down and scoop Ella Mae into his arms. He cradled her against his left shoulder, then offered Miriam his right hand to help her stand up.

She hadn't thought Amish men were particularly strong when he'd offered his hand, but once she'd locked hers in his grip, she rethought that stance. Helping her stand while steadying Ella Mae steady hadn't affected him at all. The muscles in his forearm tightened. She kept her gaze away from his biceps. Checking them out would not be appropriate.

A thought flashed through her mind. She checked her left hand. She had a baby, but no rings.

"Am I married?"

"I don't know if you are. You still use the name Miriam Troyer. I didn't see any rings, so I assumed you were divorced."

Or never married. She heard the judgment in his tone.

Divorced. She didn't like the sound of that. The Amish didn't divorce. However, having a child without being married also wasn't approved of. So which was she?

If she'd left her husband, his mother would not like that. But then—

"What if I am divorced and my ex-husband is chasing me?"

Sergeant Yates pulled out his smartphone. "Divorce records are public record. We should be able to check that out."

She nodded and watched him tap his phone for a moment. Then Sergeant Yates frowned at the device. "Y'all have zero service out here," he complained to Caleb. "I can make calls, but I can't access the internet. I will see what I can find once I'm back to civilization and let you know everything I've learned tomorrow. What time can you be there?"

"I'll be done with the chores by eight. I will have to rearrange a couple of appointments. How about nine thirty?"

Miriam left them to make their plans. She needed to act while Ella Mae was cooperating. She scurried around the room, making sure she had everything that had been removed from her bag. Although she didn't think they'd taken out much, it was better to be thorough. She searched her backpack quickly for a phone but came up empty-handed. Either she didn't have a phone or she'd left it somewhere.

She was a coward. Caleb was waiting for her to take her to his house, and Sergeant Yates had agreed to remain until they left to make sure they got out safely.

And she was holding them up because she was nervous to sit in a buggy with Caleb.

Ridiculous. He would not pay her any attention. He was doing what he saw as his Christian duty to assist someone in need. That was it.

She zipped up the side pocket of the backpack and prayed for safety for all of them and for Lucas to make a full recovery.

Whether that meant she lived a life of faith normally, she

wasn't sure. She liked to think she did. Mostly because it would put one more piece in the puzzle of her life and be another clue to who she was.

Hopefully, tomorrow Sergeant Yates would be able to illuminate more details from her life. Maybe he'd even tell her she had a safe place to go. She wondered where she'd been headed when her car ran out of gas.

Was there someone waiting for her and Ella Mae who would worry when they didn't arrive? Maybe by the time she met with the police someone would have reported her missing. That might at least tell her who her friends were.

"Miriam? Are you ready?"

Miriam jumped, startled. She'd been so deep in thought, she never heard Caleb enter the room. The idea of letting him see her rattled unsettled her, so she smoothed out her expression before spinning to face him.

"I'm ready."

She didn't relish the idea of carrying the car seat and her bag to the buggy. It would be a struggle, but she'd already put him in an awkward situation. Caleb was doing far more for her than many would. Actually, probably more than he really wanted to. The last thing she wanted to do was to ask him for assistance.

She placed Ella Mae in the car seat. The infant began to cry and fuss, kicking her legs in protest. Miriam fished inside the backpack, drew a pacifier out of the baggy she'd seen earlier and gave one to Ella Mae. Once the child fisted the pacifier and lifted it to her mouth, Miriam fastened the chest restraint. She stood and hoisted the backpack over the shoulder of her uninjured arm. Leaning to keep the bag from slipping off her arm, she reached down to grab the car seat.

"Here. Let me get that for you." Caleb swooped in and lifted the car seat. "We will go out the back door, *ja*?"

She nodded, relieved that he'd stepped forward, even though she'd refused to ask for help. Truth be told, she would have found it difficult to carry the baby and the bag at the same time, especially with the extra bulk of the carrier.

Now that he was toting her daughter, she felt silly for her stubborn resistance.

"I'll leave first. Wait a few minutes to see if anyone follows me, then you can go." Sergeant Yates loped to his cruiser and hopped in.

Caleb carried Ella Mae to a buggy and opened the door. He set the car seat on the floor of the buggy, then held out a hand to assist Miriam inside. Miriam stepped inside the buggy, releasing his hand the moment both feet touched the floor. She didn't want to acknowledge the spark of attraction that passed between them.

The awareness shadowing his expression hinted he was fighting the same thing.

Even if she wasn't married, she didn't know who she was. Romance in her situation was the last thing on her mind. And with someone like him? Out of the question. She wasn't Amish; hadn't been for a long time. The odds of someone like him leaving the Amish community were slim to none. The likelihood that she would reject the *Englisch* world and return to her family was just as weak.

Why wasn't Caleb climbing in, she turned to see him giving her a strange look.

"You can't sit there. Sorry. You need to stay down," Caleb reminded her, gesturing to where she sat on hard wooden seat inside the buggy.

Heat flooded her face. She'd been so caught up in her own thoughts, she'd sat on the bench without thought.

"Oh. Right. I forgot." Anyone looking at the buggy head-on would see her sitting behind Caleb. She arranged herself cross-legged on the floor, glad she was wearing flexible jeans.

It wasn't comfortable. It would be worse once Caleb urged the mare to trot. All that bouncing and jolting while she sat on a hard floor would not be fun.

But it would keep her and Ella Mae alive. That was the point. No matter how uncomfortable it was, she promised herself she would not complain.

Caleb was trying to protect them. If he'd left her to her own devices, she and her daughter would have been killed when their pursuer made his second trip around. Instead, two good men had been shot. And Caleb was opening his own home to her, risking his safety and the welfare of his family.

She would not forget what she owed him, no matter what.

Caleb waited until Miriam settled herself on the floor and gave him a thumbs-up before closing the door and climbing onto the front bench. It felt awkward, knowing she was behind him and he was supposed to act like he was on his own.

"Can I ask you something?" Her voice floated up from the floor behind him.

"*Ja.* But we shouldn't talk once I move. It will look strange if I talk with no one in the buggy with me."

"I've been so confused with everything. But I remember you saying something about my father. Do I have a family? Anyone I still talk to?"

He grimaced. He'd hoped they could avoid that topic for now.

"You have a sister, Beth. She and my sister Molly married two of the Bender brothers." He nearly rolled his eyes. She would not remember the Bender family, either.

Sergeant Yates began pulling out of the driveway.

"The sergeant is moving. We have to go in a minute."

"I understand. Tell me quickly then, what about the rest of the family? You said you were sorry about my dad?"

This was not the time to tell this story. But if he hedged or said to wait, she'd worry herself into a lather while they drove. He would be better off quickly telling it.

"You mother died when you were younger. You and Beth were raised by your *daed*. He never remarried. About four and a half years ago, there was a fire. Your father was killed. I'm sorry."

It was more convoluted than that. Someone had burned down the family's auction barn and shot her father. Amos Troyer had been a *gut* man. He hadn't deserved to die that way. Still, that was a conversation for another day.

He picked up the reins and flicked his wrist, urging the mare to a walk. Once they were on the street, he'd allow her to trot. He braced himself for the sound of tears. When she didn't burst into noisy sobs, he allowed himself a single glance back.

Then wished he hadn't.

He'd never seen someone look so lost. The haunted look in her eyes would linger in his memory for the rest of his life, he was sure of it. Silent tears dripped down Miriam's face. She pressed her lips together. Was she trying to keep quiet?

That alone told him she wasn't the same attention-seeking *maidel* he'd known so long ago. That Miriam would have taken advantage of any opportunity to get sympathy.

At the end of the driveway, Sergeant Yates turned his

police cruiser right, heading toward town. Caleb turned the mare and buggy left, toward his own *haus*. Although he'd never been one to rely on the *Englisch* police, he wished he'd bought a home closer to town so he'd be able to legitimately follow the sergeant. It might be safer.

Ack! Where was his faith? He didn't need to follow the police. *Gott* was with him.

Setting his jaw, he flicked the reins again. The mare launched into a trot. Caleb braced his feet against the floor to remain stable when the buggy swayed. He heard a knock behind him, then a soft voice said, "Ouch!"

Biting his lip to keep from laughing, he ignored Miriam's mutters. When Ella Mae mewed, Miriam shushed her. The *boppli*'s agitation never morphed into crying.

Relieved, he relaxed on the bench. Miriam was a *gut* mother. Shaking his head in wonder, he stopped at a stop sign, then continued when the way was clear.

How would he explain the day's events to his mother and sister? He had no doubt she'd be *welkum* into his home. His mother was well-known for her hospitality. The drunk driver had put her in a wheelchair and made pain a daily presence for her, but he hadn't changed the purity of her heart or her love of her family.

He needed to emulate her better. She would not have been happy with his attitude toward Miriam earlier.

He tensed again when an engine roared up behind him. A quick glance in his side mirror told him his worst fear closing in on him. A green truck swerved in and out of his mirror.

He had no doubt it was the man who'd shot the doctor and Lucas. Was he here to finish the job?

"Miriam." He tried to talk without moving his lips. Her

name came out barely recognizable, but it was the best he could do.

"Caleb?" her startled voice responded. He had told her that they could not talk.

"The truck is behind me."

He wasn't sure what he expected her to do with that information. She was already down and out of sight. She had no phone to call for help. They could not stop and run from the buggy. The old mare would never be able to outrun a truck on the road.

Miriam murmured in the back seat. He frowned. Why was she talking to him? Then he caught a couple of words. She wasn't talking to him. She was praying.

Would he ever stop underestimating her?

The truck moved into the passing lane. Caleb's hands tightened into fists around the reins.

"Stay down. He's in the passing lane."

He could not say anything more. The truck was beside him. The window slid down. A bead of sweat rolled down Caleb's neck and was absorbed into the collar of his shirt.

"Excuse me."

Swallowing, he glanced over at the truck keeping pace with him. The driver wore a pair of dark sunglasses and a baseball cap. He also wore a thin surgical mask. The kind Caleb had seen *Englisch* wearing around town a time or two.

There was no way he'd be able to describe this man to the police, if he got the chance.

"*Ja?* Can I help you?"

Be courteous. Don't let him know you think he's a killer.

"Maybe. I'm looking for my wife and daughter. She called me and said her car broke down and she's walking to a gas station. Have you seen her?"

"What does she look like?"

"Blond hair. Blue eyes. Pretty."

"I'm sorry. I can't help you." Caleb doubted that Miriam would have married this man. "You said she had your daughter with her? How old is your *kind*? Oh, and what's her name?"

The man hesitated. "About a year. And her name is… Ellen."

Definitely not his daughter.

"I'm sorry. I haven't seen her. Maybe you should go to the police and file a report, *ja*?"

Had any Amish man ever told an *Englischer* to get the law involved? He was experiencing all kinds of firsts today. He almost wished the lying villain beside him went to the police. They were looking for him. Sergeant Yates would have him arrested and in a cell in no time at all and then they could find a way to get Miriam safely back to her life.

Whatever that would mean for her.

In the meantime, he had to convince the man who'd murdered a friend and had tried to do the same with Lucas, a young woman and an innocent *kind,* that he had no idea what he'd done so Caleb could get Miriam and Ella Mae to safety

If Caleb had been standing on the ground instead of riding in his buggy, he would have taken a step back. Rage vibrated from the man in the truck like an angry black cloud. He might have even said it was creepy because he could not see the man's eyes or his face. Yet he knew that he was in the presence of a killer.

"I'll keep that in mind," the man told him, his words clipped.

The window rolled up and the truck sped off, spinning up dirt and gravel. A couple of rocks hit the plate glass shield protecting the buggy driver and any inhabitants. As the truck zoomed back into the right lane, clouds of exhaust fumes nearly choked Caleb.

The moment the truck was out of sight, he loosened his grip on the reins and wilted back against his seat. They'd survived that encounter. But they could not stay here.

The truck may come back around. Or the man may figure out that Caleb had misled him.

"Thank you," Miriam whispered. "I'm sorry you were forced to lie for me."

"I didn't lie. He asked if I'd seen his wife and his one-year-old daughter, Ellen. He never said your name. I've not seen a one-year-old named Ellen."

"I don't think he'll stop, either."

He had the same fear.

SEVEN

It was past dinnertime when Caleb directed the mare to ease the buggy into the barn at his *haus*. Rhoda waved to him as he pulled in. She had wheeled *Mamm* onto the front deck he'd built soon after they had moved in. *Mamm* enjoyed sitting out there in the evening, watching the sun go down as the day ended. The summer months were her favorite. She claimed she could smell the flowers blooming.

The trees surrounding the *haus* hugged it with their shade, providing the one-story ranch home with enough shade to keep it cool on days when the temperature soared into the nineties.

After parking the buggy, he helped Miriam out, then paused. "My *mamm* and my sister are out on the front porch. I don't want to take you that way, though. It may be better to go in the back door and ask them to join us."

She sent him an agitated look. "Do you suppose he suspected I was in the buggy?"

He shrugged. "Doubtful? But I don't think he'll stop searching. He's been determined up to this point. Let's not let our guard down now."

She nodded. Then began to reach for Ella Mae. He blocked her with his arm. "Let me. It will be safer for you to get out of sight. Why don't you wait for us on the porch?"

He pointed at the three steps and small four-by-six porch off the back door. There was a wheelchair ramp built off to the side. He had constructed that, too, with the help of his brothers-in-law. In fact, he'd made sure the entire *haus* was structured so his mother could move around with ease despite being confined to a wheelchair. It gave them all joy to see her thrive.

Miriam hesitated for a moment, then she lowered her hands and moved to stand as directed. She bypassed the ramp and climbed the steps, moving back into the shadows. He could still see her, but her face was partially obscured. He preferred to be able to see her, so he had an inkling what thoughts were circling about inside her head.

When had he ever really understood her, though?

Caleb hid the grin struggling to break free. Miriam had always hated being told what to do. It seemed that, at least, had not changed since she'd left the community.

Once he was sure Miriam was out of sight of anyone driving along the road searching for her, Caleb reached to get Ella Mae. He caught the handle of the carrier and swung it toward him, setting it near the door just inside carriage portion of the buggy. The baby stared at him for a moment before her little lips curled into a tiny smile. Then she gave him a wide-mouthed grin, showcasing her two bottom teeth. She gurgled at him, waving her arms at kicking her tiny feet.

My, she was adorable. How could one not smile in the face such cuteness? Without realizing what he was doing he captured her feet in his hands and grinned when she laughed.

From the porch, Miriam chuckled. The warm sound ran along his nerve endings. The hair on his arms stood on end. He'd been annoyed with her earlier and had forgotten how dangerous a beautiful woman like Miriam could be.

He could not forget. She had developed a reputation as a heartbreaker before she left. He was not interested in adding his name to the list of those who had fallen for her.

But when he glanced her way, she wasn't paying any attention to him. After steeling himself to be strong and resist her lure, it was a bit disappointing that she didn't even seem aware of him. All her attention was on Ella Mae. When the little girl caught sight of her *mamm*, her giggles exploded. He carried the car seat in the *haus* and went back for her backpack.

Climbing the steps with the bag in hand, he paused on the threshold when Miriam began to sing. He'd never heard her sing before, not even when they were kids. Her soft, lilting alto mesmerized him. Quietly entering the room behind her, he smiled at the lovely picture she made, holding her daughter in her arms and swaying from side to side while she sang.

The floor creaked under his feet. He flushed. He'd forgotten about the loose board.

Miriam stopped singing and glanced at him over her shoulder. "Oh, good. I need to feed her."

The baby kicked and squealed. Miriam rolled her blue eyes. "Yes, Ella Mae, we know that you know those words. Look at you, getting all excited."

She tickled her belly.

Suddenly, he was struck by the amount of love Miriam had showed Ella Mae, even though she didn't remember her.

"Do you recall anything?" he blurted.

She paused. "I hadn't thought of it, we've been so busy trying to avoid getting killed. I don't remember much. But there are times when something occurs to me and I realize

I know it. Like when I opened the bag this afternoon, and I knew that this kiddo is okay with baby cereal, hates peas with a passion, but will devour sweet potatoes and carrots. Or I know that my favorite color is green. Little things. I remembered that song, but I don't know where I learned it."

"It was a *gut* song."

Caleb whirled to find his *mamm* and Rhoda in the doorway, their expressions curious. Now that the moment arrived, he wasn't quite sure how to introduce her to his family. *Mamm*'s expression, while friendly, was also guarded. He knew why. He'd never brought a woman home before, and now he'd brought an *Englischer*. He could only imagine the thoughts racing through her mind.

Miriam's happy air of playfulness vanished. She moved back so she was standing behind his right shoulder. That shook him out of his frozen state. No matter what else was said about her, the Miriam he'd known had been fearless. She'd take on any challenge, accept any dare.

This timid church mouse of a woman barely resembled the girl from his memories. What had happened to dampen that wild spirit?

Maybe it was *gut* that she'd learned some restraint. But to see it totally diminished saddened him far more than he would have expected.

"*Mamm*, Rhoda. Sorry I missed dinner tonight."

Rhoda's eyes were huge as they bounced between Caleb, Miriam and Ella Mae. She bit her lip. He thought she wanted to ask who Miriam was, but his sister was too polite to do that. Her gaze snagged on Ella Mae and stayed for a full twenty seconds before she returned to him. He could not blame her. Ella Mae was an adorable *boppli*.

Mamm grew tired of waiting for someone to speak. "Caleb? Will you introduce your friend, my *sohn*?"

"*Ja*. Actually, *Mamm*, you know her. This is Miriam Troyer. You remember Amos Troyer's Miriam? Miriam, this is my mother Esther and my sister Rhoda."

The guarded expression gave way to surprise. Sorrow flashed across her face. "*Ack*, Miriam. I remember you. I am sorry about your father."

"Thank you." Miriam dipped her head. "I don't remember him."

Mamm started in her wheelchair. "You don't remember your father? How can this be?"

Caleb winced. He'd be explaining in far more detail much sooner than he planned.

Miriam hadn't meant to blurt out that she didn't remember her dad. She'd been flustered to find Caleb's mother and sister watching them. Plus, something about the way his mother studied her unnerved her. It was like she was trying to decide if she needed to hide the family silver.

She recalled what Caleb had said about her as a child. If Caleb had known her, his mother would have known her, as well. Had she liked Miriam? Or would she be upset to have someone like her in the house?

Miriam had reacted to the perceived judgment by going on the offensive.

That hadn't worked out well. Caleb looked like he might be regretting bringing her into his home. She needed to make this better. Taking a deep breath, she fixed a smile on her face. The goal wasn't to lie or be charming, but rather to tell her story well enough that she and her daughter could stay the night until she went to talk with the police in the morning.

"I'm sorry. I didn't mean that the way it sounded. Also, I apologize that we sprung this on you so suddenly. Today has been a really hard day. I wasn't being sassy. I really can't recall my father."

Ella Mae began to whimper. That caught his mother's attention right away. "Does that poor thing need to eat?"

She nodded her head. "Yes. I have formula and some cereal in my backpack."

"Rhoda, grab the high chair we use for your sisters' *kinder.*"

Rhoda hurried away. Soon, thumping sounds came from the next room. "Sorry. It was stuck in the closet."

Miriam grabbed the backpack, found Ella Mae's teething cookies, and pulled one out. Her daughter began pounding the tray with her hands. "Ma-ma-ma!"

"Oh!" Miriam dropped the bag. "She said my name."

Caleb grinned at her. "I've not heard that yet."

"I don't know if she's said it before." Some of her frustration leaked into her voice. "I think it's the first time, but even if not, it's the first time I recall, so I'm going with it."

Leaning over, she inhaled her daughter's sweet scent, then kissed her forehead. "Ellie Bean, can you say 'Mama' again?"

The little girl whined. Miriam smiled. If she'd said it once, she'd say it again. Funny how such a simple thing could rejuvenate her good spirits. She'd started to get used to Caleb's rather brusque, but surprisingly sweet personality. Coming into his house, though, had erased the comfortable feeling.

She wanted his mother to like her. Of course, she did. After all, she was depending on the woman's hospitality, at least for the night.

But it was more than that. She wanted Esther and Rhoda to like her because they were important to Caleb.

While she watched her little girl make a mess of the

cookie, the tray, and herself, she told the other women about the events of the past day, starting with waking up in Lucas's field with a sore arm and Caleb kneeling beside her.

"Someone tried to run you over?" The older woman was horrified.

She bit her lip. "Yes. He also came back. Lucas was shot, and—"

For some reason she had trouble telling them about the doctor. Caleb took over the story when he saw her difficulty. "*Mamm*, Dr. Spade was killed."

"That poor man!"

By the time the story had been revealed, Ella Mae had finished her cookie and was beginning to nod off at the table. Miriam washed her up and cleaned her gums. Rhoda showed her to a room where a crib was already set up for when the grandchildren visited. Grateful, she changed Ella Mae and lay her down to sleep. She suspected Ella Mae was getting to the stage where she fought bedtime as if it was a personal affront. Tonight, she was so tired, she went straight to sleep nearly the second her head settled against the mattress, with its fresh scented sheets.

Miriam wanted nothing more than to join her. Her body ached, she barely could keep her eyes open, and she felt grimy and disgusting.

When someone knocked on her door, she opened it to find Rhoda standing there, holding a clean dress. "*Mamm* thought you may want to clean up and get into some fresh clothes. These belong to my sister Abigail. She's about your height."

Grateful, Miriam gathered the clothes. She nearly cried when Rhoda informed her they had running water. "I think if it were just him, Caleb would have foregone the plumbing, but it's easier for *Mamm*. He'd do anything to make her happy."

Maybe it was her imagination, but Miriam sensed a warning hidden in Rhoda's words. *Don't get too attached to my brother. He won't do anything that mother won't approve of.* She ignored the implied message and smiled her thanks for the clothing. She was so tired, maybe she'd been mistaken. Regardless, Miriam wasn't here for romance. Nor did she intend to stay. Tomorrow, Caleb would bring her to the police station. She'd learn about her life and find a way back to it, then her association with these people would end.

The sadness accompanying the thought surprised her.

Shaking off the feeling, she thanked Rhoda and moved back into the room, shutting the door so she could change.

Leaning back against the door, she surveyed the room. The walls were bare of any décor, and there were no curtains on the windows. Strangely, she felt at ease in these surroundings, even though, according to Caleb, it had been more than a decade since she'd last stepped foot inside an Amish house. She shrugged and changed into the dress. Even that felt natural.

Rhoda had included a *kapp* with the dress. Miriam's hand hovered over it. Should she? She felt like a fraud. She was no longer Amish. The shorter hair brushing her shoulders confirmed that. She set it on the dresser, along with her old clothes.

The bed looked so tempting. But if she lied down, even for a few minutes, she might not get up again. That would be rude, and she didn't want to embarrass Caleb or offend her hostess.

Sighing, she said a quick prayer for strength and wisdom, then walked back down the hall and into the kitchen, where she found Rhoda and Esther talking quietly. Standing in the doorway, she noted for the first time that all the countertops were lower than normal. Esther maneuvered her wheelchair around like a pro, gathering what she needed and placing it on her lap, then wheeling to the table to put it there.

She studied the fine workmanship of the surfaces and ran a hand along the smooth top of the counter nearest to her position. "Caleb made these, didn't he?"

Esther sent her a sunny smile. "*Ja*. My *sohn* has a gift. He wanted me to be independent in my own home."

That was what a loving son would do.

Caleb strode into the room. He'd cleaned up, as well. He saw her and stopped, as if his feet had been glued to the floor. "That's Abby's dress."

Did he not approve?

"Your mother lent it to me. My clothes…"

"*Ack. Ja.* They need to be cleaned."

Miriam planned to burn that outfit when she went home. After today, that outfit forever would be associated with blood and death.

Esther and Caleb talked quietly about the day's events. Every so often, Miriam added a comment, but mostly she listened. The way Caleb listened to his mother impressed her. Esther Shultz spoke in unhurried, measured tones. Yet he never seemed impatient.

When it was time to prep for the evening meal, Miriam was surprised how much time had passed. She offered her assistance. With a smile, Esther shook her head.

"You relax. You're exhausted."

Rhoda and Esther assembled a light meal of cold cuts, cheese, and fruit. Miriam built a sandwich with ham, cheese, lettuce and a light layer of mayonnaise on home-made bread. When she took a bite, she hummed with delight. She hadn't realized how hungry she'd been.

"I know it's not fancy," Rhoda told her, gesturing at the food.

"It's better not to heat up the *haus* this late at night," Esther added. "Tomorrow will be hot and humid, after all the rain today. We keep the windows open at night to cool the *haus*, then in the morning we'll shut them to keep out the heat."

"This is delicious," Miriam assured them sincerely.

Miriam ate her sandwich and fruit, then pushed her plate back. Rhoda stood quietly and left the room. She returned a minute later.

"I went into your room and took your clothes from earlier," Rhoda told her. "If we wash them tonight, maybe they will be dry enough to wear in the morning."

She'd be sad to put them back on. But she could not go around pretending to be Amish.

"Thanks. I'm hoping that tomorrow, Sergeant Yates will tell me more about my life and when I can return to it."

"Not until it's safe," Caleb cautioned. "You can't bring Ella Mae into danger."

She nodded, tamping down her irritation. She'd already thought of that.

"You'll leave her here," Esther declared. "She'll be safe with me and Rhoda. You'll be able to accomplish more if you don't have her with you."

She knew it was true. That didn't stop panic from lancing through her heart. Leave her little girl?

"It will be *gut*," Caleb assured her. "She will be watched and well-tended."

She'd been run over and shot at, had hidden inside a buggy like a stowaway, yet nothing thrown at her up to this point distressed her like knowing she would be leaving her baby with strangers.

Caleb left his place at the table and moved to her side. Placing his hand on the back of her chair for support, he squatted next to her.

"Miriam." His soft voice compelled her to meet his eyes. "Tomorrow will be wonderful hard. You may find out who is after you, maybe you'll learn if you are married or divorced, or maybe you'll discover something else unsettling. Won't you feel better knowing that Ella Mae will be out of harm's way?"

She could not speak around the emotion begging to be released. Her body was a pressure cooker, ready to burst with everything she was keeping bottled up. If she opened her mouth, who knew what would come out?

"Miriam, you don't know us—" Esther leaned over and took Miriam's hand in hers with a strong grip "—but we will watch Ella Mae as if she were our own *boppli*."

Boppli. That meant baby.

Despite her efforts, a tear escaped. If she didn't leave now, she'd disgrace herself. She stood. "Thank you. I'm tired. Would you think me rude if I went to bed?"

The last word wobbled.

Caleb rose from his chair. "Good night. I will see you in the morning."

She fled back to her room, the tears falling before she closed her door.

EIGHT

The sunlight peeked over the horizon. Caleb left his room and padded to the kitchen to start a pot of strong black coffee. He'd need it to get through today.

He shoved his feet into tall work boots and carried his steaming mug to the barn. This was his favorite time of day. Those first moments when the day was new and filled with possibilities. He'd do the morning chores and spend some quiet time alone with *Gott*. When he went back to the *haus*, his *mamm* and sister would be stirring, bustling around the kitchen or doing their morning chores.

Would Miriam be awake? Did she rise early in the morning, or did she tend to sleep late, rising when the sun was higher in the sky?

Although, if she slept in today it would be *gut*. Yesterday had been brutal.

He frowned, recalling her struggling to remain composed after dinner. He'd seen the tears she'd tried to hide as she'd escaped to the bedroom she used. Today would be difficult, but the new Miriam he saw impressed him. She didn't scream, pout or try to flirt her way out of trouble. She tended to be direct in her approach. And she didn't expect others to get her out of trouble.

Caleb completed his chores and returned to the *haus*.

He left his mud boots at the back door and sauntered into the kitchen. To his surprise, Miriam was awake. She was chatting with his family while feeding Ella Mae. That *kind* had all three women in her thrall. He chuckled under his breath. If he was honest with himself, she had him, too.

Ella Mae chucked her baby spoon to the floor. Clucking her tongue, Miriam stood and crossed the room to clean it in the sink. He was disappointed to see her in her jeans and shirt from the day before.

Shoving the ridiculous thought from his mind, he kissed his mother on the cheek and sat down to eat breakfast with the women.

"What time will you leave?" Rhoda took a bite of a blueberry muffin.

He held up a finger, chewing his own sweet mouthful, then washed it down with a swig of piping hot coffee. "Sergeant Yates wants us there by nine thirty, ain't so?"

He shifted to face Miriam.

"That's right. Would it…" She bit her lip. He ducked his head to keep from staring.

"What?"

"I was wondering if we could stop by the hospital to check on Lucas."

His eyebrows rose. She didn't know Lucas that well. That she would show such concern for his friend showed true depth of character. "*Ja.* I wanted to ask you if we could stop, anyway."

She smiled. He gulped down a larger sip of coffee than he intended. It burned his throat. He choked and fisted his chest.

He needed to leave the table before he embarrassed himself. "I have some work to complete. We should leave here by eight forty-five."

That should give him enough time to get his mind in the right place. Caleb went to his room to finish getting ready. It took him longer than normal. When he realized he was wasting time to avoid being in the same room as Miriam, he scoffed at himself. He was acting like a child instead of an adult in his thirties. He could handle being alone with Miriam, especially since she wasn't someone whom he'd ever be tempted to get involved with.

Well, he might be tempted. In fact, he was.

But he certainly would not allow himself to fall for her. First, she might be divorced. He doubted she was married. Though he knew she had wondered. Surely, as an *Englischer*, if she'd been married, she'd wear a wedding ring. Or at least he'd have seen some indication, like an indentation in her finger. *Nee*, he felt confident that she had no husband. Which left him wondering if she'd been divorced or a single mom.

He would not judge, either way.

Except, he had judged her yesterday. It hadn't been his right to do so. Ashamed, he bowed his head and promised to do better. To be the kind of man *Gott* wanted him to be.

The other reason he could never allow himself to fall in love with Miriam, and this went to the core of who he was and what he believed, was that she had left the Amish church. Granted, she'd never been baptized, so it was permitted for her to retain her relationships within the community. But Caleb knew for him, *Gott* must always *cumme* first. No matter how beautiful, or strong, or fascinating a woman was, he would never allow himself to act on any feelings if she didn't share his faith.

What would be the point?

His chest ached. He would love to one day have a family. Ella Mae came to mind.

He needed to go. It would not help to dwell on what he could not have.

When he returned to the kitchen, he found his mother sitting alone. "Where's Miriam? We need to be leaving soon."

"*Ja.* She's changing Ella Mae. She'll be here soon." His *mamm* fixed a narrowed-eye stare on him. "She's pretty. And a wonderful *gut mamm.*"

He sighed. He'd hoped he could stop thinking about her *gut* qualities for a few minutes. Apparently, he was wrong. "*Ja.* I know. But I also know that she is not Amish. Don't worry, *Mamm.* I know what I'm doing."

Maybe so. Asking her to *cumme* home with him had been the right thing to do. He recalled Dr. Spade's counsel to protect the innocent. At the time, he'd only thought about Ella Mae. What *boppli* wasn't an innocent? He admitted he'd had suspicions regarding Miriam and about what she might have done to put them into such extreme circumstances.

That was yesterday. The past day had taught him she was a woman of good character, so different than who she'd been previously. Could amnesia change someone's personality?

He didn't know much about the condition. However, he did know that Ella Mae adored her mother, and the feeling was mutual.

Nee, he could not believe she'd changed that much because she could not remember.

He would stand firm and protect them both to the best of his ability. While he was a pacifist at heart, and would never pick up a gun or weapon for any reason other than to hunt, Caleb would put his life on the line if needed.

He would trust *Gott* to take care of him and his family.

Footsteps echoed on the wooden floor in the hall outside the kitchen. He turned with a polite smile on his face, then froze. It took considerable work to maintain his smile.

Miriam strode into the kitchen, all feminine confidence this morning. She'd brushed her hair until it shone like golden silk and the hopelessness that had dimmed her light the night before had been conquered by a defiant gleam in her eyes. She wore none of the cosmetics the *Englisch* liked to use, and she didn't need them.

Miriam Troyer was a queen among women, at least in his mind.

She aimed a fierce smile at him. She was ready to do battle.

"I'll meet you at the back door," he told her, desperate to escape his mother's scrutiny. "Please wait until the buggy is ready to *cumme* out."

She held up a small pillow. He hadn't even noticed it. "I will. Rhoda gave me this so the floor would not be so uncomfortable to sit on. Wasn't that thoughtful?"

"*Ja*. Rhoda is very kind."

Not having to sit next to Miriam would help. He would not have to look at her or talk with her. He would be able to keep his distance. He hoped.

She started talking to his mother. "Ella Mae will be ready for a nap…"

The door closed on their conversation. He hurried to the barn. He'd taken up too much time this morning. Now, he had to hurry so they would not be late. Caleb abhorred arriving late. His friends and acquaintances often commented that if Caleb Schultz said a meeting began at nine, if you walked in at five minutes after nine, you were six minutes late.

Not today. For the first time in his adult life, he ran the risk of being late.

And it was all because of Miriam Troyer.

By the time he had the buggy harnessed and ready to go, she stood directly inside the back door watching, her fingers drumming on the window. He glanced at the road. Not seeing anyone, he motioned her to *cumme.*

The back door opened. Inside, a *boppli* wailed. Her steps faltered. Then she firmed her mouth into a straight, determined line and marched to his side. He opened the door and helped her climb inside, inhaling the lemony scent lingering in her hair when it brushed his face.

He had to hold his breath. It was that or lean in to take another whiff.

He waited until she placed the pillow on the floor, sat, and gave him a thumbs-up. After closing the door, he made his way to the driver's bench and picked up the reins. One thought ran in a loop through his brain.

He was in deep trouble.

Despite the rather flat pillow Rhoda provided, riding on the floor of the buggy remained uncomfortable. Every jolt and vibration traveled up Miriam's spine. Within five minutes, her jaw hurt from the way the clattering motion made her teeth chatter. She had to clench them to keep them from knocking against each other.

Now her teeth stopped rattling, but her jaw ached.

This was going to be a long day.

If only they could talk to take her mind off her bruises and pains. But she could not distract Caleb. To this point, the killer, whoever he was, didn't seem to know she had left with the solemn Amish man.

It wasn't clear why he'd shot at Lucas and the doctor. She slammed her lids closed at the memory. She would not blame herself, but neither man deserved to be shot. Why would anyone choose violence?

A little smile escaped. Part of her Amish upbringing might have been coming through.

It was nine twenty-five when Caleb maneuvered the docile mare into the parking lot of the Sutter Springs Police Department. From where she sat behind him, Miriam heard him muttering to himself, complaining about how late they were.

"We're not late." Miriam rolled her eyes. "We've still got five minutes before we said we'd be here. We have plenty of time."

Caleb stepped down from his bench. He opened the door to the buggy and stood there scowling at her. She resisted the urge to reach out and push her finger against the ridges of his furrowed forehead to smooth them out.

"We told him we'd meet with him in five minutes. That means we should have arrived at least ten minutes ago to give ourselves some wiggle room. We still need to walk in and let the receptionist know we're here."

"Okay?" Miriam shrugged at him. It wasn't a big deal. But she decided it wasn't a good idea to voice that thought. Caleb had his grumpy face on again. Yesterday, that face bothered her. Today, she found it adorable. Bouncing around in the back of that buggy must have done something to her thinking.

After closing the door, Caleb motioned for her to go ahead of him, his eyes scanning the parking lot and street. No doubt searching for signs of the man in the green truck. She shivered. When Caleb touched her elbow in a protective gesture, an electric shock zinged up her arm.

She jumped, pulling away.

He flushed and stepped away from her. "Sorry. Didn't mean to offend you."

Her face heated like it had been set on fire. "You didn't. I got some kind of shock. Sorry for overreacting."

He didn't reach out to touch her again. She was glad. Right?

Her emotions tangled inside her. She could not decipher what she felt. To cover her unease, she began to chatter to him.

"Miriam."

She stopped talking and looked at him. "Yeah?"

"It's okay to be silent. I know you're confused. Life's thrown a lot at you. I'll talk to you if you need to talk. But don't feel you have to. I'm *gut*."

"I don't know why I'm talking so much. I am just so nervous about this. With technology, I'm pretty sure Sergeant Yates will have my whole story. And I'm not sure I'll like who I am."

There, she'd said it.

"Then change."

"What?"

Caleb sent her a smile, not the plastic one he'd worn when his mom was watching, but a real, warm smile. "Miriam, we always have ability to improve. *Gott* made us to grow and become like Him. If you don't like something about yourself, then change it."

"That's not easy."

"*Nee*, change never is. But if something never changes, it dies."

She didn't want to think of anything dying. But he had a point. She believed God had a plan for her, and she wanted to be a good person, a role model for her daughter. Someone she could be proud of.

Was she doing that?

She sank into silence, allowing herself a few moments to breathe and prepare for what they would learn.

At the front desk, Caleb gave the receptionist their names. "We have an appointment with Sergeant Yates."

"Please have a seat. I'll let him know you've arrived."

Miriam veered for the corner chair, the one farthest from the door. Caleb followed her. When he sat down and stretched his long legs in front of him, she observed him for a moment. He wasn't talkative, or an extrovert who exuded friendliness. But there was something comforting about his presence. She went back and thought about his rant about punctuality.

That was Caleb in a nutshell. He did what he'd promised, when he promised to do it. He respected other people, and their time. He wasn't overly warm, but he was there when it counted, a staunch friend and ally.

Did she have anyone like that in her life?

Somehow, she felt the answer would disappoint her.

"Mr. Schultz, Miss Troyer? Sergeant Yates is ready to see you."

They stood. An officer opened the door and held it for them as they entered. He led them through the department. She wasn't sure what she expected. But the simple room with a dozen or so desks wasn't it. Some had officers sitting at them. Others were empty. A couple of officers stood around a coffee center along the far wall.

The officer led them out of the main room down the hall to a conference room. Sergeant Yates sat at the large rectangular table with another officer.

"Steve," Caleb greeted the other man, his voice equal parts surprise and pleasure. "I didn't think you'd be back this soon."

"Nice to see you, bro. Yeah, we got back early. When Allen here told me about the case, I asked if I could join you."

He eyed Miriam. She squirmed, not liking being put under a microscope.

Caleb scratched his chin. "Miriam, this is Lieutenant Steve Beck. Hmm…"

"It's a little convoluted," Steve laughed. "In a nutshell, I'm sort of related to Caleb, and sort of related to you."

Her eyes widened. "How is that?"

She knew her family had been Amish. How would she be related to a cop?

"Let me explain. My wife, Joss, is the sister of Gideon and Zeke Bender."

She didn't respond.

"I forgot, you don't remember your past. Your sister, Beth, married Gideon."

She nodded. "So you're Beth's brother-in-law."

"Exactly. And Caleb's sister married Zeke Bender." Steve and Caleb exchanged a questioning glance.

"Enough. You guys aren't telling me everything."

"Sit down," Sergeant Yates told her. "We have a ton of information. Some may be hard for you to hear. Ask any questions if you don't understand."

Her leg bounced under the table. They were dragging this out too long. "Fine. I get it."

She winced at her abruptness, but she needed to get a handle on her life.

Caleb sent her a sympathetic glance. "It's *gut*, Miriam. We are here for you."

"Appreciate it. I just hate being in limbo. You know?"

"I get it," Steve told her. "My wife had a time when she found out some stressful things about her childhood."

Suddenly, she gasped.

"What?" all three men yelled.

"Bender. I remember the name. I remember someone saying something about wishing their twin had been found. I don't know who. It's a male voice."

Caleb and Steve looked shocked. "That was Gideon, the youngest Bender sibling. He was talking about my wife. Joss had gone missing when they were toddlers."

"Gideon… Gideon…" She squeezed her eyes shut. In her mind, a face with a quirky grin formed. She knew that man. Funny. A practical joker. So scary brilliant he intimidated her.

"I broke his heart," she blurted, aghast.

"You did," Steve acknowledged, his voice kind. She opened her eyes and stared at him, horrified. "That was a long time ago. He and Beth are happy. They have a little boy. Samuel. He's a year and a half. And will soon be a big brother."

Caleb's ears turned bright red. Why was he embarrassed? Then it clicked. Ah, yes. Amish don't talk openly about pregnancy.

"What else should I know?" She didn't want to think about hurting someone. Some instinct inside told her she'd done it maliciously. And she also knew, although she didn't recall everything, that she'd hurt her sister when she discarded Gideon. What kind of person did that? Was she still like that?

"Right." Sergeant Yates shuffled some papers. "I have all this information digitally, but I copied some of it for you because I thought it may help you remember."

That was sweet.

"The first thing you need to know is that you are a widow."

She blinked. "I'm a widow? I'm only thirty-two. Did he die in an accident or get sick?"

"Unfortunately, no. This is your husband." Sergeant Yates set a picture in front of her. An extremely good-looking man with a casual air about him grinned at her. His smile told her he knew he was handsome.

"I didn't trust him," she said slowly, pulling the words out from deep in her soul. "Why?"

"Timothy Barnes, age thirty-seven. From the information I gathered, you married him about six months after you started working in the same store he managed. He was a pharmacist. His family had been well off, so he tended to live well. But he wasn't satisfied. My sources say he stole the drugs he had access to and sold them with a partner, Owen McCallister. Mr. McCallister murdered him. We don't know why. Even while on trial, he refused to say a word. You walked in on him after he killed your husband and testified against him. It was your testimony, in fact, that convinced the jury to find him guilty on all counts. But before he went to jail, he escaped."

He set another picture in front of her, then lifted his fingers away as if the picture was a snake he expected to strike.

Miriam shook her head at the nonsensical thought. It was only a picture. She was being ridiculous. She took a deep breath and looked down at the cold-eyed killer who'd murdered her spouse and then come after her and her sweet baby.

She exploded from her seat, screaming, as memories detonated inside her brain.

NINE

She could not breathe!

Spots blocked out her vision. She felt herself falling… falling…

"Miriam! Wake up, Miriam!"

Voices called her name through a long tunnel. She tried to bat them away, but they kept calling, one of them standing out above the others. For some reason she could not ignore it. It was insistent, and something about it promised safety.

She pulled herself up through the sea of cotton weighing her down.

Opening her eyes, she saw Steve and Sergeant Yates on one side of her. Caleb sat on the floor next to her on her other side. She blinked away the remaining cobwebs.

"You remember," Caleb said. It wasn't a question. He gently touched her hand. It was the only warmth she felt. The rest of her body shivered, chilled down to her very soul.

"I did. I remembered everything." Now, she wished she hadn't. Some things were better left in the past. She shuddered so hard, her teeth chattered.

"Get her a blanket," Steve said to Sergeant Yates. Immediately, the younger man hopped up and ran to get one. When he returned, they draped the blanket over her. She realized Steve had elevated her legs.

They thought she was going into shock. She just might be, too. What she'd remembered…well, it was more than anyone should ever see. She squeezed her eyes tight against the memories pounding in her head.

The three men remained quiet, waiting for her to regain her equilibrium. After a few minutes, five at the most, her stomach settled. Heat coursed through her body. She shoved aside the blanket.

"Miriam, do you think you can get up now?" Steve held out a hand as if to help her up.

"I think so." Feeling ridiculous on the floor, she started to rise. Caleb shifted and supported her with an arm around her back. When she felt steady, she took Steve's proffered hand and rose to her feet. Then she shook off their hands and walked unsteadily back to the table by her own power. She could do this. Caleb held the chair for her and she lowered herself as if she might break apart at any moment.

Every second, she felt stronger.

The three men backed away from her seat, all of them ready to leap forward and catch her if she so much as sneezed. If she'd been evil, she'd pretend to feel weak just to watch the entertainment. That would not be kind, though, so she sat and behaved herself.

Catching sight of the picture that had caused her swoon ripped away her amusement. She tapped a shaking forefinger on the image. "This is the man who came after me."

Sergeant Yates sighed. "We were afraid of that. For some reason, Owen McCallister is fixated on you."

"It makes no sense," Steve interjected. "If you think about it, his cousins, who are still at large, broke him out of a prison truck, killed the armed guards, and then disappeared. McCallister has to know if he goes after you and gets caught, he'll never get out again. You can identify him."

"If I die…"

Beside her, Caleb swallowed loudly.

"If you die, he's the first one on our radar. He risks getting put back in the slammer forever. He's never struck me as unintelligent."

"We don't know what his motive is, though," Sergeant Yates said. He leaned forward and folded his hands on the table. "Take us through it. What do you remember?"

"Okay. Let me think a bit." She thought about starting with the day she arrived home, but she wanted Caleb to hear the whole story. So he could see the trajectory of her life. "I'm going to start at the beginning. I know you two—" she indicated the two law-enforcement officers at the table "—know most of this, but I need to tell it all to do it right."

She waited for them to acknowledge that they were willing to hear the long version. They nodded.

"As you know, I grew up in the Sutter Springs Amish community. When it was close to the time I needed to decide if I was going to be baptized, I got cold feet. I was young, brash, and hungry to see the world.

"I realized quickly that the world wasn't as I thought it would be. I became disenchanted and regretted my hasty decisions. I even thought I could come back to the Amish world. But I was afraid no one would accept me the way I was. When I heard my father died a few years ago, I went into a bit of a tailspin. I couldn't even come back for the funeral, I was so deep inside my own grief. That's when I met Tim. He seemed to be everything I wanted and he swept me off my feet. It didn't take long before I realized he wasn't what I thought. Who I thought."

She clenched her hands together under the table. She

could do this. Discreetly, Caleb reached out and wrapped his warm hand around hers. His strength bolstered her courage.

"I started to see signs that he wasn't being honest with me. He started buying things that I didn't think we could afford. The apartment we lived in was far more lavish than his salary should have allowed. At first, I thought he'd gotten money from his parents. When we went to their house for a weekend, his father gave him the third degree about saving money and being responsible. I realized they hadn't given him a dime. It wasn't until I got pregnant that I realized things had to change."

Caleb squirmed in his seat and removed his hand. She snickered and glanced at him. His ears and cheeks glowed red. Was it wrong of her to think he was adorable when he got flustered?

He refused to meet her eyes. She took pity on him.

"Do you need to go out in the hall while I talk?" She wasn't kidding. Even though she found his discomfort amusing, the last thing she wanted to do was to make him feel uneasy. Caleb had done so much for her, she didn't want to abuse his feelings.

"I'll stay," he replied, his voice gritty.

His willingness to remain even while uncomfortable warmed her heart and soul. He was a good man. Why hadn't she found someone like him before she ruined her life?

Steve cleared his throat.

"I started to suspect that he was doing something illegal. I knew from our shared checking account there wasn't enough going in there to keep up our lifestyle. Or rather, the lifestyle he forced us into. A pharmacist and a cleaning lady could make a decent living, but not a lavish one.

"Drugs did enter my mind. So did a few other crimes. But I didn't have any proof. I heard a suspicious phone call, but it wasn't explicit enough to be sure he'd started dealing drugs. However, I was not going to raise a child with a criminal for a father. I didn't think he would care if I left. He'd never shown any inclination to be a dad. But by that time I was a little afraid of him. So I saved some money on the side, and I made plans to leave him in secret. I had a new debit card. Before I could leave him, Owen McAllister killed him in our apartment one day. I walked in on it, and he would have killed me, too, if I hadn't run out screaming into the street."

She looked Caleb straight in the eyes. "I was the reason he was sentenced to sixty years in prison. I testified against him. As you heard, he escaped. When I heard this, I left the city and moved to a small, rural community. I legally changed back to my maiden name, and changed Ella Mae's name, as well. I met Dina, and we became best friends. She was the one who invited me to church. But Ella Mae is the reason I gave my life over to Christ. I didn't want to be the selfish person I'd been. I wanted to be a good mom, worthy of respect."

She looked at Sergeant Yates. "Dina's dead, isn't she?"

He nodded, sadly. "I'm afraid so. When we looked you up, we found that she'd been murdered in the apartment you shared with her."

Miriam swiped angrily at the moisture on her lashes. She was sick of crying, but it seemed that was all she ever did. "I walked in on him again. Again! I knew she was dead. He came after me, but her body blocked the door. I made it to my car, but I dropped the phone in the parking lot. I got into the car and drove without a destination in mind."

"Why didn't you go to the police station?"

She shrugged at the sergeant's question. "With Ella Mae? There was no way I could have gotten her out of the car and run in before he'd caught up with me. The one day when no one was patrolling for speeders!"

"You ran out of gas," Steve said.

"Yep. Stupid, right?"

She took them through the last few minutes—seeing his truck and pushing her daughter down the hill.

When she finished, they were silent for a minute. Then Steve turned to Sergeant Yates. "Say, Allen. Did anyone find her phone?"

Sergeant Yates—she could not think of him as Allen— shook his head. "Nope. It wasn't logged in as evidence."

"Makes me think our suspect has it."

Once Sergeant Yates affirmed his statement, Steve continued. "Listen, Miriam. He's still out there. And we have to assume he's coming for you. I want you to avoid anything that can be tracked on your phone. Don't log in to email, social media, any apps you may have had. Do you have digital banking?"

She nodded.

"Don't use it. If he has your phone, he may hack it and find your location. We can get you a supply of cash for a few days."

"I'm guessing I shouldn't use my credit card or debit card, either."

Caleb frowned. "I didn't see those in your purse."

"I had hidden them deep inside my bag. I had started hiding them before I planned to leave Tim. I never got out of the habit."

"Don't use them," Sergeant Yates said. "We can find some place to put you. Until we do, I want you to stay at Caleb's house. I will plan on having unmarked cars do drive-bys. They may do a check-in."

Caleb didn't look happy about it, but he agreed.

Sergeant Yates pointed to the picture. "You take that. Show it to Caleb's family. If you reconnect with your sister, show it to her, too. You need to make sure everyone knows who is after you."

Feeling numb, she followed Caleb out and climbed back into the buggy, barely noticing the discomfort.

Tim's killer. Dina's killer. He was still out there. And he was coming for her. The universe was playing a bad joke on her, but she was no longer laughing.

What could he say?

Through the entirely of her recital, he'd experienced so many thoughts and emotions. He had been happy to see she felt remorse for her past and had decided to live a righteous life. It was wonderful *gut* she had her memories of Ella Mae. His neck flushed when he recalled her mentioning her pregnancy.

To live through what she had seen, though... Sorrow filled him. She no longer loved her husband, had said she'd feared him, but to see him, to see anyone die...

He could not finish the thought.

He wanted to bring her home. She'd be comforted when she held Ella Mae. But they'd planned to stop by the hospital first. He contemplated changing their plans. He didn't want to do that without her input, though.

"Miriam."

When she didn't respond, he glanced around to make sure no one was watching, then tried again.

"Sorry. What?"

"Hospital?" He tried not to move his lips, so it emerged without the *p* sound in the center.

"Yes. I think we should check on Lucas."

He directed his buggy toward Sutter Springs Mcmorial Hospital while contemplating how to make sure she had the least amount of exposure. "When we get there, I'm going to pull up under the carport. You need to get inside quickly. Keep your head down. There's a blue shawl on the floor of the buggy. My sister uses that sometimes instead of her black bonnet. Cover your head and shoulders with that."

She wrestled around in the back seat. He still could not see her, which was for the best.

"I found it." She was quiet for a moment, probably wrapping up her head. Every few seconds he caught a flash of a hand or blue fabric. "Don't you think it would look suspicious me coming in with a blue scarf wrapped around my head in the middle of June?"

"*Nee*. This is Amish country. These scarves are seen all over. Young and old wear them. I'm surprised you don't remember that. And a lot of *maidels* wear them with their jeans."

"Ah, I forgot. *Rumspringa*." She huffed a brief, humorless laugh. "You have to recall, I've been gone nearly half my life. I'm sure there are more things I've forgotten about than things I remembered."

A deep sadness came over him. He'd lost three years from being asleep in a coma, and he still felt a little haunted when he considered what he missed. He'd always remember waking up to Molly's voice, telling him about her marriage to Zeke. It stung that he hadn't been there to celebrate with her like he had for Abby and Betty's weddings.

And he'd be there for Rhoda's wedding someday, *Gott* willing.

"Get ready. I see the hospital ahead of us."

"Wait! Caleb! What do I do when I get inside?"

He paused. A car swerved into the turn lane. He let the

driver pass, then pulled the reins to the side to move the buggy into position.

"When you get inside, go to the waiting area. I'll join you once I park the buggy. Keep your face hidden."

Ahead of them, the Sutter Springs Memorial Hospital sprawled across half the block. The other half was taken up with various parking lots.

He'd always thought it strange that people had to pay to visit their sick loved ones in a hospital. He always parked in the short-term parking, the few times he'd been here. That was free.

The hospital had been built in several waves. The original structure was a square three-story building. Two wings had been added on either side. The front carport had been added last, along with the lobby and sliding doors. He'd always thought it was a monstrosity, but the people in Sutter Springs were proud of it.

The mare's hooves clip-clopped on the blacktop parking lot. He directed the mare to the carport and pulled the reins to stop her. She halted and stood, waiting for his next command.

Caleb hopped down and scurried around to allow Miriam to exit. She stumbled slightly. His hand reached out to catch hers. When she was stable, he squeezed her hand. "Go. Quickly."

Keeping her head down, Miriam gripped the shawl around her as if it was a sixty-degree day in October. He chuckled, then hurried to park the buggy near the very back of the lot. If anyone came looking, his buggy would not stick out immediately. Not that it would. Another buggy sat along the edge of the lot.

Most Amish used drivers to *cumme* to the hospital. Especially if they planned to stay for any length of time. However, if someone was making a quick visit while already in the area running errands, it wasn't out of the ordinary to see a lone buggy in a parking lot.

Caleb sauntered across the parking lot, trying to observe the vehicles in the surrounding area without looking like he was scanning the lot and street. He forced himself to keep his pace natural despite the urge to hurry crawling up his legs.

He'd never been so happy to arrive at hospital doors in his life. They whooshed open at his approach. Cold air smacked him in the face when he walked inside the air-conditioned lobby. He shivered as he looked around for Miriam, who was hiding in the corner of the waiting area, watching for him behind an opened magazine. He grinned. She was possibly overdoing it, but that was fine. She was being cautious. He'd rather that than running into oncoming danger.

He motioned her to wait, then went to the front desk and asked about Lucas. The receptionist barely glanced at him while she looked up his room number. A minute later, he returned to Miriam. "Room two-oh-three. Let's take the elevator."

They rode in silence. The elevator bumped to a halt and the door opened with a squeak.

"They might want to look at that," she murmured.

Caleb huffed a quiet laugh next to her. Their footsteps echoed in the hall.

"I'm surprised no one is guarding his door," she told Caleb.

He opened his mouth, then closed it again. The explanation wouldn't be comforting.

"What?"

He didn't want to speak his thoughts, but he would never lie to her. "He wasn't the target."

"Oh. Yeah. I hadn't thought of that."

Thankfully, his bluntness hadn't done any damage. She appeared a bit unsettled, but he saw no sign of impending tears. He hated seeing her cry. It made him feel useless.

Arriving at Lucas's room, Caleb rapped his knuckles on the door. Lucas's voice called out to him to enter. Unlike the rest of the hospital, his room felt warm.

"How are you, Lucas?"

"Caleb. Miriam. I want to go home."

Miriam gave him a sympathetic glance. When she removed the scarf and folded it over her arm, he started to argue with her.

"Just while we're here," she told Caleb. "It's too warm for it."

He didn't argue, but he wasn't happy about it.

"When will they let you out?" Caleb asked.

"*Ack.* They say this afternoon. I need to be checked again to make sure my wound isn't infected."

Miriam listened, her face pale. "Lucas, I'm sorry I brought this to your house."

He shook his finger at her. "You did not. You were attacked, too. Someone chose to harm me. I will forgive, so it doesn't stain my heart, but they will pay a price for their wickedness."

They only stayed a few minutes. Lucas would be fine, and he had already been in touch with family. He didn't need help.

"I'm glad we stopped," Miriam said. "He sounded like he'll be all right."

"*Ja.* Lucas will recover. I think we can stop worrying about him."

"All I want now it to go and see Ella Mae. Once I know she's okay, I'll breathe easier."

When they got to the waiting area, he held out his hand to stop her. "Wait here. I'll bring the buggy around so you don't have to cross the parking lot."

He left the hospital and headed to his buggy. Once seated, he started to pull out, but a car waiting for another vehicle to leave blocked him. The driver glanced his way once, but the moment he caught her eye, her gaze shied away. From that moment, she focused with unnatural intent on the parking space she was waiting for.

The other vehicle was taking its time to back up.

Caleb sighed and glanced up the street.

His blood froze. A green truck turned the corner and was headed down the street. In a minute, it would pass by the hospital.

Miriam wasn't known for her patience. He would not have time to drive the buggy there.

Throwing himself from the buggy, he hit the ground running.

TEN

Miriam tapped her foot on the beige-and-black checked linoleum floor as she waited inside the hospital for Caleb. She considered going out, but he had been adamant that she remain inside until he'd determined it was safe for her to leave.

The door slid open. She stood tall, prepared to leave. Instead of Caleb, Sergeant Yates entered. She blinked at him. He grinned, although she saw the weariness in his posture.

"I didn't expect to see you here," she blurted.

"I could say the same. However, I thought I'd check in on Lucas while I was coming this way. I saw Caleb in the lot. Don't go too close to the door. I can stay with you?"

She shook her head, not wanting to delay him.

"Okay. But I will only be a few minutes. If you need me, have the receptionist page me." He walked away.

Sighing, she crossed her arms then glanced at the clock above the receptionist's head. Five minutes had passed. It wasn't that big of a parking lot. He should have been here at least two minutes ago.

Maybe if she left the waiting area and went to stand in the lobby area near the sliding doors. Just far enough so she could see Caleb. She moved forward. Stopped.

No. She needed to wait. She bit her thumbnail, trying

to resist the pull of the glass doors. She hated not knowing what was happening.

She stood firm in her decision for all of thirty seconds. Then her imagination started to crank out scenarios. Owen McCallister running down Caleb. Or a car backing up into his buggy. Or him falling off the buggy, bumping his head, and lying unconscious in the middle of the parking lot.

Each image grew worse.

She had to see if he needed her. Then she'd go back into the hospital and wait, exactly as he'd asked her to. If she was careful, he would never know she didn't follow his directions to the letter.

Moving past the reception desk, she approached the first set of sliding doors. Her stomach dipped when she walked through them, reminiscent of the sensation of riding in a car down a steep incline too fast. Silly. She wasn't going outside. She was just checking on Caleb.

She approached the second set of doors, stopping before the motion detector activated so they didn't open. Narrowing her eyes, she squinted deep into the parking lot to find Caleb. He ought to be easy to spot. Buggies tended to stand out.

Way in the back corner, she saw the buggy. It was blocked by a couple of cars. Stretching up on her tiptoes, she attempted to see Caleb. When that failed, she sighed. He'd come when he those cars moved.

She wanted to get back to her daughter. Ella Mae had reached the stage where if Miriam left her sight for more than a few minutes, she cried. Though she settled down after ten minutes or so.

At least she'd regained the memories of her precious daughter.

Still, it hurt to think of the sweet little girl crying because her mom left. If it was up to her, Miriam would never leave her daughter with others.

She'd grown up without a mom. Now that her memories had returned, she recalled loneliness and isolation. *Daed* had dealt with the loss by becoming increasingly strict. No singings until they were seventeen, which was older than any of her friends had needed to wait. No hanging out with boys, ever. Except for Gideon. He allowed him because Gideon and Beth had been friends since they were in diapers. They did everything together. In time, Miriam did what many teenage girls did. She rebelled, every way she could. Looking back, Miriam wondered how she'd stayed as long as she did.

Then Gideon and Beth grew old enough to go to singings.

Amos Troyer never saw the moment that Beth's feelings toward Gideon shifted and became a full-blown crush. Miriam did, though. Jealousy ripped through her. Miriam grew up knowing she had her mother's beauty and charm. Boys always watched her, flirted with her.

But *Daed* didn't allow them near her.

Beth, however, had Gideon with her all the time. Gideon was handsome, funny, quirky, and smart.

Miriam hadn't cared about that. What bothered her was her sister had a boy hanging around, and she had feelings for him. And Miriam had no one.

It wouldn't be long, she knew, before he began to notice Beth. Then she did what no sister should ever do to another. She set out to entrance Gideon. For all his brilliance, he never saw the manipulation for what it was. It had been rather easy to snare his attention. Once he'd fallen for her, people expected an engagement announcement. Worse, Gideon started talking of marriage and a family.

He wanted her to agree to be baptized and join the church before he proposed.

She couldn't commit her life to the church. Or him.

So she left and broke his heart.

Miriam cleared her mind of the memories. That Miriam no longer existed.

Just when she had decided to return to the waiting area until Caleb came to get her, an elderly woman hobbled up the sidewalk, leaning heavily on a cane. Arrested by the sight, Miriam stood a few feet from the entrance, praying for the woman to make it the last little bit.

"Come on, you can do it."

The woman's wrinkled hand wobbled on the head of her cane. She bumped into the curb of the sidewalk, and the cane fell on the blacktop driveway. The woman faltered. If she bent down to pick it up, she might fall. But she could not continue without the aid of the cane.

Before she thought better of it, Miriam flew out the door and picked up the cane. She handed it back to the woman.

"Thank you, my dear. I don't know what I would have done if you hadn't come along."

"You're welcome."

Miriam watched her to make sure she made it the rest of the way inside the building. As the sliding glass doors whooshed closed behind her, she heard her name.

Spinning, she saw Caleb sprinting toward her. He was halfway across the lot.

He hadn't been greeting her but had screamed a warning. Too late, she saw the green truck on the street. When the window rolled down, Miriam bolted to the side.

Crack!

The first bullet went wide and hit the potted plant beside her, smashing the clay pot to smithereens.

The second bullet caught Miriam in the side, burning a path along her rib cage.

She'd been shot, again.

Caleb saw Miriam go down and hurtled toward her, his heart pounding.

Police officers and security piled from the building, surrounding Miriam. Sergeant Yates ran out, gun raised, and shot at the green truck, hitting the side above the rear wheel. The engine roared. Smoke billowed from the twin tailpipes. The truck raced down the street.

Sergeant Yates ran out into the parking lot, yelling into the radio on his shoulder, and jumped into his cruiser. Within seconds, the cruiser surged from the parking lot, lights flashing and sirens blaring. The traffic on the street pulled to the side to allow him to pass.

In less than ten seconds, both vehicles had disappeared from his view. A second cruiser, siren wailing, rushed by.

Would they catch him time?

A crowd surrounded Miriam, concealing her. Cameras flashed. Excited chatter filled the air, reminding Caleb of the squawking of geese. Everyone talked over each other.

"Miriam!" He shoved his way past the nosy bystanders and dropped to his knees beside her. "Miriam."

"Hey, Caleb." She grunted. A stretcher was brought out. "No! I just got out of this place. Now I have to go back in?"

A red stain blurred across the side of her shirt. He blanched. "You are hurt."

She nodded and groaned again. "Yeah. He got me and the plant."

"What?"

Her hand flapped in the direction of the wall. For the first time, he noticed shards of pottery littering the ground.

His mind was so scattered, the only thought that emerged was someone needed to clean that up. Even as it crossed his mind, he knew it to be ridiculous.

The paramedics loaded her up on a stretcher. Panic flared in her eyes.

"Caleb!" Her hand reached for him. When he grabbed her hand, her breathing slowed and she relaxed back against the stretcher. "Don't leave me."

"I won't."

They wheeled her into the emergency room. The doctor on call came in almost immediately. Caleb had never heard of that happening. Normally, people talked about waiting for hours before the doctor saw them.

"You were fortunate, young lady."

"I don't feel fortunate. I feel like I got shot."

Caleb could not help the smile that worked its way across his face. Even after a shooter had nipped her, Miriam remained spunky. Her feisty attitude was one of her main attractions. More than her physical beauty, which was fleeting. *Nee*, Miriam had an untamable spirit, one that would survive the trials that life threw at her.

The doctor smirked at her. "When I say fortunate, I wasn't referring to your getting shot. Obviously, that is the antithesis of fortunate."

She snickered. "Obviously. Then what were you talking about? Because I could really use some good news here."

"The bullet grazed your skin, but there's no depth to the wound. So while it bled quite a bit, now that it's slowed, we'll bandage it and let you go. Change the dressing twice a day for the next two days and keep it clean."

She nodded fervently. "I can do that."

"I'm going to write a prescription for a strong pain medication."

She made a face. Caleb doubted she'd take the medication, but she didn't protest when the doctor typed away on his laptop.

"When did you last have a tetanus shot?"

She blinked. "I don't think I've ever had one."

That startled him. "How is that possible?"

She bit a fingernail and considered him. "Well, I was raised Amish, so I never went to public school. And I have not had the need since I left. I haven't stepped on nails or poked myself with a rusty metal stake. So I've never thought about it."

"Think about it now. You are getting a tetanus shot." He gave her a stern stare when she opened her mouth. She closed her lips while he informed the nurse what he wanted. When the woman returned with the necessary supplies and told Miriam to lift her sleeve, she rolled up her T-shirt and watched while the nurse wiped a small area with an alcohol pad. A second later, she looked away when the nurse primed the needle. Caleb crept a step closer in case she was scared of needles and fainted.

"You'll feel a pinch," the nurse warned.

Miriam kept quiet and although her mouth tightened when the needle pierced her skin, she didn't faint or protest.

"Good," the doctor said. "Contact us if you have any complications."

He left and another nurse entered with a laptop and a clipboard with several printed pages. "I have your discharge instructions and your script. It's a little backward, but I need to go through your registration paperwork."

Caleb rolled his eyes. It seemed irrelevant to register someone for something that had already happened. When she came to the part about insurance, Miriam frowned.

"I have a card in my wallet. I didn't bring it."

The nurse pursed her lips. "We can look it up, but I really need to get a photocopy the card for our files."

Miriam bit her lip and glanced toward Caleb way.

"This should be an easy issue to solve," he assured the nurse. Then he turned and met Miriam's gaze. "Your bag is at the *haus*. We can bring it in tomorrow. Or Monday."

"Just bring it to the front desk and tell them to copy it into her file and have them email me." The nurse pointed at her name on the bottom of the discharge packet.

As soon as she went through the instructions and Miriam signed on the highlighted line, they were on their way back to his *haus*. They didn't talk the entire trip home. He waited until they were safe inside his *haus* and his *mamm* had the chance to fuss over Miriam to begin the conversation that had been lurking in his head since the shooter got her.

"Miriam." He helped her lower Ella Mae into the high chair. "I think I know why he shot you. You weren't wearing the scarf."

Her eyes widened. She paused in the middle of spooning some plums into Ella Mae's mouth until the *kind* objected loudly. Hurrying the spoon on its way, she turned to him. "You're right. I forgot to put it on because I was focused on helping the woman who'd dropped her cane."

"In retrospect, I think it's better that you weren't seen with me. I hate that you got shot, but if he'd seen us together, he would know you were hiding with me."

"He doesn't know who you are."

"Yet. There are ways he could figure it out."

She frowned. "What am I supposed to do? How am I supposed to hide from him?"

"I have an idea. I think you should dress Amish while you are with us."

"Completely?"

"*Ja. Kapp*, too. If you do that, maybe he won't recognize you."

She gnawed on her lip. Unwilling to watch that distracting action, he turned to his mother. "What do you think, *Mamm*?"

"I think it's a wonderful *gut* idea, Caleb. She can use Abby's clothes."

A police cruiser pulled into the driveway. Caleb recognized Steve's number. "Steve's here, *Mamm*."

Her expression lit up. "Rhoda, get a plate with a couple of my cinnamon rolls for him."

Steve had no sooner sat at the table than a plate of the sweet treats and a cup of black coffee landed in front of him. "This is the real reason I come here," he joked. "Esther makes the best cinnamon rolls."

"Don't let your wife hear you say that." Caleb warned him.

Steve snorted. "Are you kidding? Joss says it, too."

While Steve ate his cinnamon roll, Caleb relayed their plan. Steve nodded. "We'll still do drive-bys. I think today was a fluke. A potentially deadly one. I want you two to use more caution from now on."

Miriam rubbed her side. "I wonder if I should just return home."

ELEVEN

Caleb felt like he'd been kicked in the chest. He hadn't been prepared to think of that option. It disturbed him how little he liked it. Only the day before, he'd been ready to ship her home at the first possible moment. Somehow, overnight, he had changed his mind. Now, he wanted to think of ways to convince her to stay.

He needed to take care. Miriam Troyer was a beautiful woman and a fine mother. She had a will of iron and so much courage that she amazed him. Her compassion touched his soul. She had shown his mother respect and had put herself at risk to help a woman who had dropped her cane.

Even now, he was certain her wish to go home had more to do with protecting his family than any real desire to return.

All that aside, she wasn't Amish. No matter how his heart pounded in her presence, or how his breathing hitched when her scent reached his nose, he could never allow it to go further. Even if it meant remaining single for the rest of his life.

"Miriam, as long as that man is searching for you, you and Ella Mae are in danger. I think you are better off here, where Steve and Allen can help us keep you safe."

"I will add to that." Steve rocked back on his chair. "Your

apartment is still a crime scene. Even if I thought you should go back, you can't go there. I've already told you that you should not use any of the money sources available to you."

Her shoulders slumped. "I hate being a burden."

"*Nee*, you are not a burden," Esther proclaimed.

Miriam shook her head. "But I brought danger to your house. I am another mouth to feed, and I am going to be using your daughter's clothes. I'm like a giant parasite!"

Caleb couldn't help it. He threw back his head and laughed. "A parasite?"

She crossed her arms over her chest. "I'm glad I amuse you."

"I don't mean to laugh. It sounded funny. I will tell you the same thing *Mamm* has said. You are not an imposition. We enjoy having you here and are glad to be able to assist."

She stopped arguing, but Caleb was sure she remained far from convinced. The rest of the day passed without incident. Rhoda and *Mamm* could be heard talking and laughing with Miriam and Ella Mae. Especially Ella Mae. It was no secret that *mamm*'s favorite days were those when the *kinder* visited. Molly and Zeke had five *kinder*, including a set of twins, Abby's little boy had recently turned one, and Betty had a little girl about three weeks old.

Every few months, *Mamm* would give him a subtle hint that she expected him to settle down and marry. Caleb did his best to deflect those hints. He'd never met anyone that he could see himself marrying.

Until now.

Shocked, he stopped in his tracks. In the other room, Miriam laughed, the sound dancing along his nerve endings. She might have been born Amish but Miriam had lived in the *Englisch* world for more than a decade. A match between them was off the table.

Later that night, he got into bed, still feeling unsettled from the spontaneous thought. He'd try to put the notion out of his mind during the evening. But lying in bed that night, his musings had free access to prey on him.

Caleb rolled over in bed, groaning. The sunlight streamed through his windows, taunting him. All he wanted was to pull the covers back over his head and sleep for another two hours.

He didn't have that option. As the man of the family, Caleb had chores that could not be skipped. Huffing his impatience, he flipped his blankets back and swung his legs over the edge of the bed.

The cold floor against his bare feet woke him further. He dressed and got ready for the day. In the kitchen, he made his coffee extra strong. He'd need every drop of caffeine this morning. Sipping the hot brew, he smacked his lips.

Then he got into his boots and headed to the barn.

By the time he returned, the woman had all risen.

"What are we doing today?" Miriam asked him, sipping from her own mug of coffee. If it could still be called coffee. He'd watched, fascinated, as she'd dumped two teaspoons of sugar in the mug. At least a fourth of the cup had been filled with cream.

"I have some chores around the farm. After lunch, we can take those discharge papers into the hospital."

"Will you call a driver?" *Mamm* asked.

He thought about it. "It's not that far. But it may be easier, rather than having Miriam crouch in the back again."

Miriam's eyebrows shot up. "Would it matter?" She waved a hand at the green dress and white *kapp* she wore. "Per your instructions, I am dressed Plain today."

He fought another smile. She might be dressed Plain,

but she still sounded persnickety and *Englisch*. *Per your instructions*. Who talked like that?

"We'll see. I'd have to go to the community phone to call, anyway. We can do that later this morning. Will you stay here or join me while I do chores?"

Mamm gave him a look. Why had he invited her along? It might have had something to do with the anxious pucker between her eyebrows. She'd work herself up into a tizzy without something to occupy her mind. Still, he thought she'd choose to stay with the other women and her daughter.

To his surprise, she opted to go with him, leaving Ella Mae in the capable hands of his mother. After donning some heavy mud boots, they headed toward the back fence, where several boards had broken during a storm.

"I have needed to spend some time outside." She tilted her head back to get some sun on her face. "You got the condensed version of my life yesterday, but I never did ask you the same. Now that I remember knowing you when we were kids, I'm curious. What about you? What happened in your life? I would have expected you to be married by now. Most men your age are."

He paused, his hammer lifted in midswing. He wanted to refuse to answer. But he saw no malice in her face. She was interested in his life. He'd be rude not to respond.

Plus, he wanted her to know. He didn't analyze that thought too deeply. He'd tell her what happened, as concisely and unemotionally as possible.

"It's a bit of a sad story. A few years after you left, a drunk driver plowed through a church picnic. My *daed* was killed. So was Molly's fiancé and half a dozen other people." She gasped. "My *mamm* ended up in a wheelchair. Molly's leg was broken in a couple places. She still walks with a limp."

"Oh, Caleb. How did you get through it?"

"I had the easy part then. I was in a coma for three years." He tried to make light of it. But the truth was, those missing years haunted him.

Miriam seared him with a level stare. "You did not have the easy part. I got my memories back, but I felt disorientated and out of sync with everything while they were gone."

He should have known she'd understand.

"I am so sorry you went through that," she stated. "No wonder you are so determined to protect me and Ella Mae. I didn't appreciate it as much as I should have. Thank you."

He waved away her gratitude. He hadn't wanted it, or her pity when he'd told her about the accident.

"So will you stay?"

She hesitated. "You were right before. It isn't safe to go back. And as much as I hate putting your family out, I can't risk Ella Mae. She's my priority. So I guess my answer is yes, we'll stay."

He didn't complain or argue again about her not inconveniencing them. She had a stubborn streak a mile wide. If she thought staying here would make him happy, he would go along with it and ease the conversation to a different topic before she changed her mind.

She turned to stare at the horizon. When she spoke, he had to strain to hear her. "I never realized how much I would miss my *daed*. Growing up, all I thought about was how strict he was or how he never let me do what I wanted. It never occurred to me that if I ever wanted to come back, he'd be gone. He'd always been there. It makes me angry that someone killed him."

"I was angry, too. But I had to let it go. I had to forgive. It was eating me up inside. I started to get an ulcer, I was so angry and bitter all the time."

She sighed. "I've been praying about it. It's not easy, but somehow God will help me forgive. I do believe that. I'm just not there yet. I admire you."

She gave him far more credit than he deserved.

"I'm not that special. I think most people around here would act the same."

She smiled. "You keep telling yourself that."

She couldn't believe all the complaining she'd done around Caleb. He had not said a word about everything his family had been through. She had figured that his *daed* had died. She had no clue about the magnitude of the story. To lose your father, a friend, and have your mother injured so badly was horrid. But to lose three years of your life! She couldn't imagine.

When he came out of the coma, had he felt like he was out of step with his friends? She asked him.

"I'm not sure what you mean."

"Did you feel like you were no longer at the same level? Like they had matured, while you stayed behind."

"Oh, sure." He shrugged. "It's better now that everyone is an adult. But *ja*, it was hard the first few years."

That topic stayed with her the rest of the morning. Sometimes she still felt out of step with her peer group. Except in the *Englisch* world, it wasn't as much about how old you were, or what grade you were in. It was all about morals and the things she would allow herself to do with things she would not. The more she prayed, the closer she got to the Lord, the less leeway she offered herself.

Of course, the friends she ran with didn't want anything to do with her once she wasn't "fun" anymore. Although they weren't mean, they stopped calling. The few times she did hang out with one of her old crowd, the conversation had felt forced and awkward. Soon, all contact stopped. Only Dina kept in touch with her.

That afternoon after lunch, Steve again pulled into the driveway.

"Two days in a row?" Caleb greeted him as Steve stepped out of the cruiser and shut the door. "This is some kind of record. Since you married Joss, I'd grown accustomed to seeing you once every month or so. This is the third time in two days."

Miriam figured that since his sister had married Joss's brother, they were sometimes all at large gatherings together. She ignored a small twinge of envy at the idea of being surrounded by a loving family.

"Well, I thought this was something you would want to hear right away." Steve looked straight at her as he spoke.

Miriam held her hands together in front of her as if she was praying. That was one thing about always dresses. No pockets. She missed having pockets.

"That doesn't sound good. What do I need to hear in person?"

"Well, it seems someone is using your bank card to get to your money."

"He's trying to rob her." Caleb growled. His anger on her behalf touched her.

"It's more than that. I suspect Tim might have hidden some of the drug money in the accounts that were marked for you alone. Maybe he even started an account in your name. We'll find it, but it might take some time. I'm hoping we can locate them before Owen McCallister does."

"I do, too. That man would scare me even if he didn't have a gun." She shook her head. "I don't get it. You said he was using my bank card, but my debit card was hidden in my purse. I told you that. I found it while we were at Lucas's house."

"Let me see it."

She ran back to her room and searched her bag for the debit card. Where was it? After upending the bag onto her bed, she rifled through everything. The debit card was missing. And so was her wallet. She remembered putting the wallet aside while searching for Ella Mae's pacifier. She must have left it on the couch, where she'd been sitting. She scowled. Such a careless mistake. Well, she'd have to go and get her insurance card, anyway. Might as well go give them the bad news.

"Guys, I'm sorry. I'm almost positive that I left my wallet with my insurance card—" she looked at Caleb before switching her attention back to Steve "—and my debit card at Lucas's house."

"I thought you kept them in separate compartments?" Caleb said.

"Well, I did. But when I found them the other day, I didn't know why I did. Pretty sure I filed them into my wallet instead of putting them back in the other pocket."

Steve stood. "Let's take a drive out to Lucas's place. He's home, so he shouldn't mind."

"You want me to go?" That seemed odd.

"I do. I want you to give me a rundown of where you were when McCallister hit you. It's not likely, but maybe we can find something that will help us locate his truck. I'm also hoping to jog your memory and see if you recall anything about his truck, like part of the license-plate number."

"That would be on the back, not the front, of his truck."

"True, but maybe he had something identifiable."

She frowned. "I barely recall his truck."

"Hence why I want you along. I'll be there the whole time."

"And so will I."

Surprised, she whirled to face Caleb. Letting her stay in his house was one thing. Tagging along on the investigation was another.

The pit of her stomach dipped like she was on a roller coaster in the middle of a nosedive.

If she wasn't careful, she could fall for Caleb, hard. She had to protect her heart. She only hoped he recognized the danger, too. She'd broken one heart in her life, on purpose. She didn't want to be responsible for causing Caleb any more pain.

TWELVE

Miriam kissed her daughter on the cheek. Guilt stabbed her in the chest. She'd been gone for hours yesterday, and now she was taking off again, leaving her baby girl with strangers.

"They're not strangers," Caleb said, rejecting her idea when she told him how she felt. "They're my family, and she is comfortable with them, ain't so?"

She sighed. "I guess. I hate leaving her, though."

"*Ja*, I understand. You're her *mamm*. It's natural. What did you do before when you cleaned *hauser*?"

She made a face. He had a point, and they both knew it. "I took her to day care."

"*Ja*. And she didn't suffer, ain't so? So now, someone else will care for her until you return. I trust Steve. If he says he needs you there, then we'll go and we'll do what he needs. Besides, you need to get your insurance card, too. This will save us the trouble of calling for a driver."

"Enough!" She laughed, shaking her head. "I get it. Fine. I concede. She'll be all right with your mom and Rhoda."

"*Ja*. She will."

Shoving aside her qualms, she walked to Steve's police cruiser. When he opened the back door for her, she nodded her thanks and lowered herself into the back seat, feeling like a criminal sitting behind the see-through protective barrier between herself and the two men. Caleb met her glance. When she smiled at him, he lifted one corner of his mouth in response and stepped into the vehicle.

"I've turned on the two-way speaker, Miriam," Steve informed her, his voice popping out of a speaker rather than from in front of her. She felt like she was in the middle of a ventriloquist show.

He pulled the cruiser onto the main road. It sure was nice sitting on a real seat rather than on the floor while traveling to Lucas's house. Potholes and craters filled the back roads.

"They need to get a grater out here," she mumbled to herself.

The men in front chuckled at her remark. They carried on a quiet conversation. Miriam didn't pay attention. Her mind whirled with all she'd recalled and been through in the past few days. The one person looming large in her thoughts was Owen McCallister. She shuddered. How he'd managed to evade capture again amazed her. He'd been responsible for two more murders, plus he'd tried to kill her and Lucas. And Ella Mae. The blood froze in her veins as she thought of that man coming after her baby.

She was the target. If she could help put him away again, this time for good, Ella Mae would no longer be in danger. And they could return to their lives.

And leave Caleb and his family behind.

Her heart ached at the thought. Caleb was grumpy, stubborn, and set in his ways. But he was also kind, giving, gentle, and had a sweet sense of humor that she wouldn't have appreciated ten years ago.

Now, she did. But she wasn't Amish, despite the clothes she wore. She had rejected that world and no longer had a place in it. Her *daed* was gone, and her sister had moved on.

Would Beth allow her presence in her life again? Especially since she'd married Gideon.

Steve turned into Lucas's driveway, yanking her from her dark thoughts.

"Why is Lucas waving at us like that?" Caleb asked.

She leaned over to peer out the side window. Lucas stood on his front porch, his face a picture of anger, frustration, and defeat. Her heart sank. Something had happened, something bad.

Steve steered the cruiser into the small two-car space near the front of the house. On the way to the house, Caleb explained that the original owners had been *Englisch* and had used it as a turn-around. Several large bushes had been allowed to grow up around the spot. It would be a good hiding space if kids were playing hide-and-seek in the backyard.

She tried to open her door, but it wouldn't budge. Which made sense. The police wouldn't want their prisoner jumping out en route to the jail. Impatience zinged through her system while she waited until Caleb opened her door for her.

When she stepped out of the car, Lucas ran down the incline of the front yard to meet them.

"Lucas," Steve greeted him. "Is something wrong?"

"Ja!" He nodded his head so hard his straw hat began to slide off. His hand flew up to catch it before it hit the ground. "I stayed at my brother's *haus* last night. He dropped me off here an hour ago. I walked in and found my *haus* was a mess. Every room on the first floor."

"A mess?" Caleb's eyes narrowed.

She recalled his neat-as-a-pin house. A wave of nausea rolled through her. Caleb edged closer to her so their arms touched. Warmth flowed through her, though nausea still roiled her stomach.

"Someone ransacked your place?" Steve's kind face morphed into a professional mask. Even without his uniform, his whole being said he was a cop.

"*Ja.* It's wonderful bad. The back door has piles of stuff around it. I can barely move in the mudroom without tripping. The kitchen's not too bad. Why would someone do this?"

She knew. They were after her.

"That's how they got your debit card," Caleb murmured beside her, unintentionally adding to her angst. Again, Lucas had suffered because of her.

Steve dipped his chin, acknowledging Caleb's words. He led Lucas back to the house. "Since you've already been all through your house, it's contaminated. I don't know that we'd get much evidence from it, but I need to call it in. I would ask that you guys stay on the front porch until we can go through it."

They all agreed. Lucas pulled a couple of chairs together, and they sat. It took another twenty minutes before Sergeant Yates appeared with a female officer. Steve introduced her as Officer Melissa McCoy. They went into the house, leaving Caleb, Lucas, and Miriam on the front porch, waiting.

She could hear them talking inside but was unable to make out any words.

After half an hour, she excused herself, telling the men she needed to use the outhouse. Caleb started to stand.

"Stay." She waved him back. "I'll be close by. And there are two police cars over there." She gestured in the direction of the turn-around.

"You can't see them from here because of the bushes."

"True, but they can see them from the road. No one will come up the driveway while they're there."

Reluctantly, he nodded. "If you're not back in five minutes, I'm coming to find you."

"Agreed." She left the front porch before he could change his mind. She just needed a few minutes alone to regain control of herself. The turmoil in her heart and mind threatened to overwhelm her, and listening to the cops inspecting a wrecked house caused because she'd been inside it fueled her agitation.

She was almost to the barn when a hand grabbed her and whirled her around.

She found herself face-to-face with Devon McCallister, one of the cousins who'd helped Owen escape. She had his picture in the file Sergeant Yates had given her. Twenty-five years old, he had been in and out of prison and had a list of jobs he'd worked until he got bored and left.

And he was a killer, just like Owen.

"The cops are here," she said, her voice louder than normal, hoping one of them would hear her.

Devon sneered. "I saw 'em pull in. That young cop and his girlfriend don't scare me. They never checked the garage, so I figured I'd wait. I have a car parked on the next road. They'll never find me."

Before he could say anything more, she wrenched her hand free and shoved the heel of her hand against his nose. Blood spurted, splattering her pristine dress and the front of his shirt. He cursed, both hands going to his broken nose.

She whirled around and took off running toward Caleb. "Caleb! Steve!"

A gunshot barked behind her. The bullet brushed her skirt and hit the ground in front of her.

She might not survive the next one.

Caleb heard her scream and bolted up from his chair. He leaped from the porch and rocketed toward Miriam.

She zoomed toward him, her face devoid of all color despite the exertion.

Behind her, a bloody-faced man raised his gun for a second shot.

"Miriam!"

Caleb caught her in his arms and enfolded her in them, then dropped to the ground, rolling so his back was an open target to the shooter.

The back door burst open so hard that it now hung sideways. Caleb watched Steve and Sergeant Yates pound out the door, their feet whipping up dust in their wake. Sergeant Yates pulled his weapon from the holster on his belt. Steve didn't bother with his gun. He took the man with a running tackle.

Both men hit the ground with a thud, sending a cloud of dirt into the air.

The man with the gun started yelling and swearing. Steve and Sergeant Yates disarmed him and yanked him to his feet. A pair of handcuffs appeared. Caleb didn't see who pulled them out. Within a minute, the man was cuffed and Sergeant Yates marched him to his cruiser, while reading him his rights.

Caleb heard the name McCallister.

He helped Miriam to her feet. Lucas joined them. The three of them watched the two cops deal with the man who'd gone after Miriam. He looked younger than the picture he'd seen at the police department.

Finaly, his heartbeat began to slow. "That wasn't Owen McCallister."

Miriam faced him, her features drawn. "No. His cousin Devon. One of the two who had been helping him. He was one of the men who assisted Owen escape on the way to prison."

Steve sauntered over. The small group watched the police car depart with Devon in the back. "We know for sure that they're working with Owen McCallister."

"What do I do?" she asked. "He saw me dressed Amish."

Steve nodded. "Yes, but his cousin didn't."

A curious expression crossed her face. "He said the young cop and his girlfriend didn't scare him."

Steve smirked at that. "I'm thinking he only saw Allen and Melissa pull in. So we are probably safe. Still, I will increase the watches on your place, Caleb. If he'll talk, which I won't count on, we could have Owen in custody this weekend. Either way, his picture has been sent to every precinct in the surrounding areas. The chief ordered locating and apprehending him as our top priority." Steve gaze sharpened. He shifted to face Miriam squarely. "We're doing all we can to get you home. If he's not found this weekend, a place has opened up. We'll hide you away somewhere else."

Caleb's gut clenched. He had two more days, then she was out of his life, again.

It was for the best.

But no matter what he told himself, he didn't believe it. When she left, she'd take his heart with her.

He'd been foolish and fallen in love with Miriam Troyer.

The rest of the day passed without incident. The police were no closer to finding either Owen McCallister or his other cousin, Gary. However, Lucas's home had been straightened up and he was able to continue his work. Caleb's family had celebrated when that announcement came through.

On Saturday, she agreed to help Caleb run some errand. For the first time, she sat in the buggy with him, keeping her head down, as if she was demure rather than hiding her face. Caleb remarked about the houses he drove past.

When they drove by Lucas's house, she could hear someone hammering away inside the house. It felt strange that no music played. Whenever she had done work in her apartment, she'd streamed music from her phone.

She hadn't missed it.

"As soon as his place is ready he'll sell it and move to a smaller home."

Miriam played with the straps of her *kapp*. "What happened to Lucas's wife?"

She knew it was a bold question. One she'd never dream of asking Lucas. But something about Caleb made her feel she could ask him such things. Caleb tended to be a little abrupt, but he rarely got offended.

"That's a sad story. I would not tell you, normally. It's not my story, *ja*? I will tell you because it's common knowledge around Sutter Springs. Everyone knew Susan. She was friendly and the best cook I've ever met. Even *Mamm* didn't make pies like Susan. When she brought pies to the local fair, every one sold. Year after year."

He turned the buggy into the church parking lot. They were delivering some quilts his mother had made for a local group. "The year before last, Susan started having stomach issues. She ignored them until Lucas insisted she see the doctor. It turned out she had stomach cancer. She died six months later."

Miriam swallowed. That was the saddest story. So many people suffered.

It didn't make sense why God allowed it. When she said so, Caleb scratched his chin and thought for a moment. She liked that he considered his answers. "*Gott* doesn't cause the evil. He lets us make our own choices. That's where all the darkness starts. The sin comes from us."

She had to think about that one for a while.

When they arrived back at the farm, Caleb went to the barn to milk the cow. He milked her twice every day. He said if he got off schedule it would be difficult to get her back on schedule.

"Miriam!" Rhoda said as she entered. "How was your field trip today."

"It was a success, of course. Everyone loved the quilts." She helped herself to a freshly made doughnut. Biting into the soft dough, she hummed with pleasure. The sugary glaze melted on her tongue. "I need to learn how to cook."

"You don't know?" Rhoda's voice rose in surprise. "You were raised Plain."

Even though she could tell she'd caught the other woman off guard, she didn't hear any judgment. She would miss that, the acceptance she'd found here. Of course, this family knew her presence was temporary.

Rhoda waited for her response.

"Beth always cooked at home." She didn't want to talk about life with Tim. Tim had rarely been home for dinner. She didn't want to cook for herself, so she ate lots of cold cereal or salads for dinner.

"I'm glad you are here. I am taking *Mamm* to visit her sister. You are *welkum* to *cumme*. But do not feel like you have to."

"Thank you for the offer. But I feel like staying in one place for the rest of today." She wanted to stay where Caleb was, if she was honest with herself. Because soon, she'd leave and never see him again.

"I understand."

She had a feeling Rhoda understood too well.

She might have gone if she had known Esther's sister. But it might have been awkward, and she didn't want the stress of meeting someone new today.

She helped Rhoda bring her things out to the car they'd hired for the trip. "We'll be back tonight. Probably after suppertime."

"Caleb and I will be fine. Have a great time."

Miriam waved at the car until it turned out of the driveway. Once Caleb's mother and sister had left, she went in to check on Ella Mae.

Opening the door of the bedroom, she screamed. Two men with dark hair and shaggy beards stood over her daughter's crib.

THIRTEEN

Caleb heard Miriam scream. He tore out of the barn and raced into the *haus*.

"Miriam!" he bellowed.

There was no answer. In the back room, a *boppli* cried. Ella Mae! Caleb dropped the pail of milk he'd carried in from the barn. It hit the floor and splattered, soaking his pant legs. The milk ran over the floor. Caleb raced down the hall and barged into the bedroom.

A man grabbed him from behind and yanked his arms behind his back.

"Don't move so fast, Amish. It would be sad if one of them died."

Another man, who was holding Ella Mae, grinned.

Sweat broke out on Caleb's neck. These two men had *cumme* into his home and were threatening Ella Mae and Miriam. He couldn't do anything to stop them. They had the guns, and the one holding him tied zip ties around his wrists. The hard plastic strips bit into his flesh.

"Should we leave the dude?"

The man holding Ella Mae pursed his lips and narrowed his eyes. "Nah. Let's take him. It might be interesting."

They forced Miriam to walk down the stairs first. Caleb knew it took all her courage to walk ahead, where she couldn't see what was happening with her daughter. At the bottom of the stairs the taller man gave her a hard nudge when she paused. She tripped down the last two steps. When she moved forward there was a slight hitch to her walk. Caleb thought she twisted her ankle.

"We're going to go nice and slow. We're all going out to the car. No one is going to try anything stupid. Maybe if you do exactly as we tell you, everyone will live to see morning."

Caleb didn't believe a word they said. They obviously had plans, evil plans, for Ella Mae. And maybe there was a reason they would keep Miriam alive.

But his death warrant had been signed the moment he stepped into that room. There was nothing they needed him for.

Silently, Caleb began to pray. He did not ask *Gott* for his own safety. Instead, he prayed that Miriam and her daughter would escape and return home unharmed. If something happened to him, he would accept that. Caleb would gladly die in order to save their lives.

The car was hidden on the road. There was no way they would have seen it from the *haus*. Miriam was forced into the back seat. They handed her Ella Mae. The taller man ordered her to keep the baby quiet, if she knew what was good for them. The shorter man hopped into the back seat with them.

"You!" The tall man pointed his gun at Caleb. "I'm going to remove the zip ties, but no funny business. I want you to drive."

Caleb blinked at him. He didn't want to die but there was no way he could comply with the man's directions.

"Didn't you hear me? I told you to get in the car and drive."

This was one of those situations where he wasn't quite sure how he was going to get out of it.

"I heard you. I'm Amish."

"Well, yeah, obviously you're Amish. So what?"

"I've never learned how to drive a car."

Maybe if he hadn't spent three years in a coma during his *Rumspringa* years, maybe he would have learned how to drive. As it was, he'd never had a need to learn.

"You're lying. Is he lying?" The shorter man turned and asked Miriam.

She swallowed.

"Many of us don't learn how to drive. We are not allowed to use things with rubber wheels. So driving a car would be out of the question."

"He doesn't drive, Gary." The shorter man complained.

Gary. So the tall man was the other cousin.

"You talk too much, brother."

The police only ever knew about two cousins helping Owen. It appeared they'd recruited a third.

"Fine. Sit here." Gary McCallister forced Caleb to sit on the passenger side. He tugged hard on his hands then zip-tied Caleb's wrists to the handle near the window.

Caleb tried not to be too obvious about it, but he twisted his hands in the confines of the zip ties. When Gary had redone the zip ties, he had not gotten them tight enough. Caleb might be able to get loose.

But what about Miriam and Ella Mae? Miriam was holding the *boppli*. Her hands were not tied or restrained in any way. It probably would not stay that way. He had a few minutes while they were driving to come up with some kind of plan. Once they stopped at their destination, though, it might not be possible to escape.

Ella Mae began to cry. Caleb's heart stopped. He prayed no one would hurt her. The poor thing was terrified.

Gary scowled and turned on the radio. With each cry, he edged the volume higher to block out the noise.

Once he was sure the man didn't intend the hurt her, Caleb continued to work on the zip ties. If he could loosen them, maybe he could slide one hand free. He wasn't sure what he was going to do, but he would take the first opportunity to free himself, Miriam and Ella Mae. Without force.

Caleb had never had his pacifist beliefs tested before. He couldn't aim a weapon at them. He couldn't fight. How would he save Miriam and her daughter?

He might have to risk his own life so they could escape. Miriam would watch over Rhoda and *Mamm*.

A movement caught his eye. Caleb cut his eyes to the side and glanced in the mirror. Miriam had her daughter in her left arm. Her right hand was lying on the door handle.

This would take speed. He nodded to show her he understood.

The shorter man grumbled. Finally, he yelled for Gary to turn the radio down. Gary scowled. "You complain too much, Billy."

Instead of turning it down, he turned it up. Billy continued to pester his older brother, who ignored him.

The car pulled up to a light. With the radio up and the shouting going on, neither man noticed the click as Caleb slipped his hand free and unlocked the door. Yanking his other hand free, he opened his door and sprang out at the same time Miriam leaped out her door. Billy tried to grab Ella Mae. He missed and grabbed an inch of Miriam's dress. She pulled it from his grasp as they ran.

They ran into the yards behind the *hauser* and kept running. They would lose the advantage of their head start once the men began running after them.

Caleb might have had one advantage the men didn't have. He knew where they were.

"Follow me."

He curved to the right and wove between several *hauser*. Hopefully, their pursuers wouldn't see where they ran. Behind him, Miriam huffed and puffed. She wasn't used to running. Ella Mae had her head pressed into her mother's neck, her little hands fisted around a clump of fabric.

The next *haus* was an old one that had been on the market for six months. No one was buying right now, so it sat empty. It looked creepy. The log-cabin siding had thick cobwebs between all the logs. The windows were so dirty, no one could see through them. When the owners had vacated, they'd left piles of garbage and unwanted debris stacked against the garage door.

No one would want to buy this place. It was the perfect spot to hide out. They would find no food here, however, or anything to drink.

Caleb knew where the former owners had hidden a key. He pulled up a stone, grabbed the old rusty key, and shook the dirt free. It still fit in the door, but he had to wiggle it to get it all the way in. Then he opened the door. Miriam and Ella Mae went in ahead of him. They moved away from the door.

"What do we do now?" she whispered.

"We wait. In a bit, I'll sneak out to use the neighbor's phone. They know me here. We'll call Steve."

"I can't go back to your house."

He sighed. "I know. You can't go back there. And you can't go home. I really hope Steve will have someplace safe you can go. I am almost out of ideas."

She opened her mouth, but he held up his hand.

In silence, they listened. Soon, they both tensed, hearing the familiar voices of the two men as they approached.

"He's not going to be happy that we lost them," Billy complained, a definite whine in his voice.

"Well, he should have come out here himself. I figure he owes us. We've done a lot for him. They can't hide forever. Do you have the picture of the baby?"

"Yeah," Billy said. "We can't make him too mad. Devon's still in jail. We need his help."

"We don't need his help. Give me the picture of the kid."

"Here. She's cute."

Gary snorted, his disdain clear.

"Let's see if we can find it. That's the one he really wants. The other two are extra."

Their voices grew softer as they moved off.

Caleb and Miriam stared at each other, their faces shocked.

"They want my baby?"

"*Ja.* It would seem they do." He couldn't imagine why. Whatever their reasoning, it couldn't be *gut.* He would willingly give his own life to keep that sweet little one safe. She'd curled up inside his heart and taken up residence there. Right next to her mother.

They waited for another half hour. He thought it was close to four when they heard a car arriving at the *haus* next door.

"That will be Jim. Wait here." He started to feel his way to the door.

"Be careful!"

Leaving them in the dark, dank *haus*, he left to find Jim.

"Caleb! You scared me, popping out of the dark like that." The older man held a hand over his heart, although a smile spread over his wrinkled face.

"Jim. I need a favor."

"Anything. You know that."

Caleb smiled. His *daed* and Jim had been friends for years. "It's not a big favor. I need to call someone."

"Make yourself at home, Caleb." Jim led the way to the front door, pulled it open, and gestured for Caleb to enter.

Caleb thanked Jim and made his way through the *haus* to the kitchen. Jim and his wife still had a landline phone. He dialed Steve's personal cell-phone number. It was a good thing the men had stopped at a light so close to a neighborhood Caleb was familiar with. His mother and sister wouldn't be home. Who knew what kind of shape they would have been in if they had to wait for someone to realize they were missing.

He shuddered, not wanting to think of it.

The phone rang three times.

"Hello?"

"Steve!" He got choked up hearing his brother-in-law's voice on the other end of the line. He had started to doubt he would ever hear it again.

"Caleb. What's wrong?"

Steve knew him well. "Some men came into my home. Gary McCallister and his younger brother, Billy. They kidnapped me, Miriam, and Ella Mae, and forced us into their car. We escaped and are hiding out in the old Piper *haus*."

"Caleb. Go back to Miriam and the baby. I am on the way." He heard keys jangling on the other end.

"Hold on." He felt Jim's hand on his shoulder. Jim took the phone from him. "Steve, come to my place."

He talked with Steve thirty more seconds, then hung up. His face was more serious than Caleb had ever seen it. "Let's go and bring the woman and child here. That place is not fit for man or beast."

He couldn't argue with him. Caleb nodded, and together, he and his father's old friend went to bring Miriam and Ella Mae over to wait for Steve.

Miriam rocked Ella Mae, trying desperately to still her baby's crying. She was terrified the men would hear her and come get them before Caleb returned. If she'd been in a familiar place, she would have walked around, but she didn't know where it was safe to step.

Her daughter needed something to eat. And she was cold and probably wet.

Tears stung the back of Miriam's eyes, but she refused to cry. "Hush, Ella Mae. Come on, Bean. Mama's here. We're waiting for Caleb."

Ella Mae continued to cry, gnawing on her tiny fist like doing so could sustain her. Miriam's own stomach had been growling nonstop for at least fifteen minutes. Just when she thought she couldn't take any more, she heard footsteps on the walk outside the door. She tensed. She didn't hear one set of footsteps, she heard two.

Had the kidnappers discovered her hiding place? What if they had found Caleb? Miriam's pulse thundered in her ears and her breathing grew rapid. If she had a safe place to set Ella Mae down, she could pick up something to use for a weapon.

"Miriam?" Caleb's voice whispered into the dark, like a beacon of hope.

She wilted back where she sat. "Here, Caleb. We're still here."

Quietly, she thanked God for preserving them from harm. Caleb returned to her side. She stood, ready to follow where he told her to go. To her surprise, he pulled her and Ella Mae into his arms and tucked them close to his heart. He set a gentle kiss on Ella Mae's head, then pressed his lips against Miriam's in a kiss as soft and fleeting as a butterfly's wings.

"I found a friend of my *daed*. We're going to his *haus* to wait for Steve."

Miriam was all too ready to leave. Caleb removed Ella Mae from her arms and held her. To her surprise, Ella Mae turned into him, her crying changing to pathetic little whimpers.

"She's hungry."

"*Ja*. I know. And she must be scared, too. But she's safe."

That was what mattered most.

Caleb introduced her to Jim. "Take my arm, ma'am. It's pretty rough terrain out here."

Miriam did as he asked.

When they moved outside, she couldn't help but shudder. As glad as she was to leave that house, she feared being out in the open. She felt like she had a target sitting in the center of her back.

She couldn't relax until they were inside the house. Jim called to his wife, a sweet-faced lady named Naomi. The moment Naomi saw Ella Mae, she tutted. "Oh, the little lamb. Come into the kitchen. I have some baby food my daughter left from the last time she was here with my grandson."

Naomi filled the silence with cheerful chatter while she heated up a bottle of formula and showed Miriam the stash of baby food. Miriam selected some cereal and sweet potatoes, and then mashed up a little banana. When Ella Mae saw the bottle coming toward her, she lunged and grabbed it with her little hands curved into claws.

The two women laughed, although Miriam wanted to cry, seeing her daughter's desperate hunger.

"Now, you sit and tend your little one," Naomi told her. "I'm going to get something for you and your man to eat."

Heat flushed her face at Naomi's mistake. Not that she didn't wonder what it would be like to have Caleb truly in her life. Her lips still tingled from the chaste kiss he'd given her. But they weren't a possibility right now.

Caleb needed a committed Amish woman. She definitely did not fit the bill. Nor was she sure she could ever return to the Amish life. She'd been gone so long, and the people she'd grown up with surely had negative memories of her.

Then again, she'd been married before. And it had not been a good experience. Did she even want to marry again?

Her blush grew hotter.

One kiss did not mean Caleb was ready to go down on one knee and propose. Not that she wanted him to. Even if she wanted to return to the Amish, she'd only become re-acquainted with him for a few days. She needed to focus on her daughter. At this point in her life, nothing else mattered except for the child nestled in her arms.

The smell of beef frying in a pan wafted past her nose. Miriam lifted her face and sniffed, her stomach growling in anticipation.

"I'd offer to help you—" she began.

"Not to worry. I have everything under control. You just feed your baby and let me get you something to eat. I hope you like cheeseburgers and salad because that's all I have on hand right now."

"That sounds perfect," Miriam said, meaning it with all her heart.

Caleb and Jim walked into the kitchen, both of them sporting big grins.

"Something smells good. Is that for us, sweetheart?" Jim

wrapped his arms around his wife's waist and gave her a noisy kiss on her cheek.

She laughed and swatted him away. "Yes, it's for you. Why don't you be a dear and set the table."

"Always! That's an easy price to pay for your cooking."

Miriam envied them the obvious affection they shared. Would she ever find that? Her gaze sought out Caleb's. When she saw the same wistfulness in his expression, her pulse thudded in her ears.

It almost made it worse, knowing she wouldn't be the only one to suffer when she left him.

Unless she stayed.

She shook off that thought the moment it edged its way into her consciousness. In another world, where she hadn't sown seeds of pain and discontent in her past, maybe she'd have a chance to return home. But outside of Caleb's family, she had a reputation that wouldn't be easy to overcome.

It was possible for people to change. She was proof of that. But it was harder to convince others that you'd done so.

Minutes later, dinner was served. Miriam had never tasted anything better. In the middle of the meal, someone knocked on the door. Naomi excused herself and came back a few seconds later, trailed by Steve.

Steve greeted his host, but then walked around the table to where Miriam was sitting. "Are you all right? Did they hurt you or Ella Mae?"

She shook her head. "We're fine. Nothing a delicious meal wouldn't solve. But I don't think we can go back to Caleb's house."

"Definitely not. Don't worry. I have a plan for that."

"Lieutenant, you're welcome to join us."

"No thank you, Naomi. I've eaten. As soon as these three have finished, I'll be taking them with me."

Miriam finished her meal and Caleb pushed back his plate. They stood and thanked Jim and Naomi for their hospitality. Miriam made special note of the address on the house. As soon as she was able, she would send them a thank-you gift. Perhaps a bowl of fruit or a gift card to a nice restaurant. Something to show how much she appreciated them coming to their aid when they needed it.

Steve helped her and Ella Mae into the back seat of his cruiser. He had taken the time to put a car seat in there. She settled her baby in the seat, adjusting the belt to fit snug and securely across her chest. Ella Mae stuck her thumb in her mouth and closed her eyes.

"What's the plan, Steve?" Caleb's low rumble drifted from the front passenger seat.

"I talked with Isaiah and Gideon. They've agreed that Miriam should stay with Beth and Gideon."

Gideon's other brothers. Miriam recalled there were four brothers. Micah had been the oldest, followed by Zeke, who'd married Caleb's sister, then Isaiah, and finally Gideon, Joss's twin.

Steve continued speaking. "Isaiah and Micah will take turns providing the guard when I can't be there. With so many tourists in town right now, our department is stretched thin, but I will do everything in my power to make sure those two girls back there are safe."

It was more than empty words. His tone carried the weight of a solemn vow.

"I hope so, Steve. They are important to me."

She sat back. It wasn't a declaration, but her heart pounded a little faster. She wanted to tell him that he was important to her, as well.

She didn't, though. First of all, because they had an audience. But also because, the way things stood, they didn't have any hope of a future together.

She couldn't remember ever having a sadder realization.

FOURTEEN

When Steve pulled into Beth and Gideon's *haus*, several cars were parked out front. Through the open barn door, she could see a buggy. Two horses, one grey and the other a dappled mare, grazed in the field beside the barn.

Steve stopped the car and both he and Caleb got out. Caleb jogged around and opened her door. He hefted the car seat out of its carriage as if he'd been dealing with *Englisch* car seats his whole life. She smiled at him. He would make a great dad one day. Sorrow filled her at the thought that she wouldn't be around to see it.

Miriam stepped from the vehicle and stood, stretching. It felt like she'd been sitting forever.

"Miriam!" Beth bounded toward her, skidding to a stop a foot away, her joyful cry giving way to hesitancy.

Miriam understood. Years ago, she had started to reach out to her sister, then pulled back. And before that, she'd hurt her baby sister dreadfully, willfully, all because of spite. They stood looking at each other, wondering how to get past it.

Miriam was tired of being alone. She had a sister she used to love more than anyone. Before her selfishness and own loneliness had made her bitter. And now, that sister was unsure of how to greet her. Enough. Closing the gap between them, she flung her arms around Beth and held tight.

Beth froze for the two longest seconds of her life. Then, with a soft cry, she melted into Miriam's hug and embraced her back. They stood together laughing and swaying, shedding copious tears.

Finally, Miriam pulled back, her shoulder drenched from Beth's tears. Beth's opposite shoulder had a similar damp spot. "Hi, sis."

Beth chuckled. "I thought you'd left forever. When you didn't *cumme* to the wedding, I thought you'd decided not to reconcile. I'm so glad to see you."

She squeezed Miriam's hand. Miriam returned the squeeze. Her heart was so full of emotion, she thought it would burst from her chest.

"I wanted to come to your wedding. But I wasn't sure I'd be welcome. I was a brat to you." That was an understatement. She'd been downright cruel. By all rights, Beth should have refused to see her, especially since her worst action had involved Gideon.

"*Ja*, you were. But you are my sister."

As hard as reuniting with Beth had been, Miriam knew the most awkward part was next. She had to face her past, and the other person she'd devastated.

Miriam turned to the man standing next to her sister, watching Beth with loving eyes. "Hi, Gideon. Thanks for letting me come here."

She wasn't sure where she stood with him. They'd walked out together, she'd abandoned him, and now he was married to Beth.

Gideon gazed at her. She had the feeling he could see directly into her heart. At last, he smiled. "Miriam. *Welkum*."

She saw Beth looking at the car seat. Joy bubbled up.

This was the one part of her past she wasn't ashamed of. She indicated the baby gnawing her fist. "This little bit of cuteness is your niece, Ella Mae. She's tuckered out. It's been an eventful day, and not in a good way."

"Ella Mae? Like the books you used to read when you thought Teacher Wilma wasn't watching?"

A blush stained her cheeks. "I didn't think you knew about that. But yes. Although, I recognize that beauty isn't a virtue."

"She looks like you," Beth said. "In the morning, you can meet our *sohn*, Samuel."

"Why are you all standing around?" a man called from the front porch. "Let's bring this party inside."

"Is that...?"

Gideon gave his happy grin. "That's my brother, Isaiah. He's back, sort of. He's not Amish, but he's a part of the family."

She allowed Beth to slide her arm through hers and pull her into the house. Seeing Isaiah, emotion tugged at her soul. Before she had fled for the Englisch world, Isaiah and Micah Bender had both left the community. That, in addition to the absence of his twin sister, had burdened Gideon's heart. Now, Isaiah Bender was back. And Steve was married to the missing sister. The only one she hadn't seen or really heard much about was Micah, the oldest Bender sibling. But according to Steve's words earlier, he too had returned.

"God's bringing everyone together," she murmured to Beth.

"*Ja*. It's wonderful *gut*."

Both women grinned, arms entwined.

Once inside, she met more of the family. Caleb kissed his sister, Molly, and reintroduced her husband, Zeke Bender.

Micah was the only Bender brother not at the reunion, but she was assured she'd meet him soon.

"Micah is a deputy US Marshal. He and his family live about an hour from here." Beth handed her a glass of water.

Miriam laughed. "An Amish family connected to a marshal, a bounty hunter, and a police officer. It sounds like pure fiction."

She felt a little jealous of her sister, being part of this big, noisy family. Then she shoved aside the feelings. As long as Beth allowed her back into her life, she had nothing to complain about.

It took a while for Miriam and Caleb to explain what had happened that day. Miriam started yawning long before they had finished. Caleb stood to leave. Steve agreed to drive him home. Caleb caught her eye and nodded his head toward the door. She got the picture. He wanted to speak privately. She murmured an excuse to Beth, then followed him to the door.

"Are you sure you will be *gut*?"

She hiked a thumb over her shoulder. "I have a whole crowd of people in there to keep us safe. Including a bounty hunter. Who would mess with Isaiah?"

Caleb laughed. It fell flat. "*Gut*. I am going home. I want to be there when *Mamm* and Rhoda return."

A desperate urge rose up inside her. "Will I see you again?"

He looked at her, a deep searching glance. "Do you want to see me again?"

She should say no. They had no future. "Yes. I do."

He nodded. "*Ja*. You will see me again. I will stop by tomorrow afternoon."

He backed up. She hoped he'd kiss her again but knew it wouldn't be smart. When he glanced at her lips, then turned and walked away, she sighed in disappointment. He did the right thing. She knew they couldn't be together. Regret stabbed her heart.

Not long after, she headed up to bed. She'd been in the room only a few minutes when Beth knocked. It was the secret knock they had made up when they were kids. It meant, "I want to talk privately."

She opened the door. "I'd know that knock anywhere."

"I hoped you'd remember it." Beth sat on the edge of the bed. "I thought I'd stay in here for a while."

Miriam sat next to her and clasped her hand. "Gideon won't mind?"

Beth shook her head. "I've been praying for you to *cumme* home for a long time. He knows what it's like to have siblings far from home."

She nodded. They talked, haltingly at first. Miriam told her sister about her conversion, her marriage, and Ella Mae, and finally about Dina and how she ended up back in Sutter Springs. Beth told her about their *daed*.

They both cried over all they had lost.

"So tell me about you and Caleb."

She sighed. "There's nothing to tell. He's Amish, I'm not."

She couldn't lie to her sister and tell her there were no feelings between them. Because in the past few days, something had definitely begun to grow. But that had to stop. They were too old to play games. "I'm not a young girl anymore. I'm a mother, and I have a man trying to kill me. Although after today, I'm worried that my baby might be in more danger. I have no room in my life for romance while she's in danger."

The playfulness fled Beth's expression. "*Ja.* I understand. She must be your priority."

Miriam averted her gaze and picked at some loose threads on the quilt.

"When they catch this man and the danger is gone? What about then?"

Ugh. She'd forgotten how determined her little sister could be. "I think you are part terrier."

Beth laughed, not at all insulted. "Maybe so, but you have not answered my question."

There would be no peace until she responded. "I don't know. It's been a long time since I left. Almost half my life. A lot has happened. I won't lead Caleb on. He's a good man, and I do have feelings for him. At the moment, that's all I know."

"I won't bug you about it anymore. I just want you to be happy."

She could not respond and say she was happy. Which concerned her. Because even while she protested about returning to the community, she wasn't sure if she could be happy without Caleb now that she'd found him.

Before she fell asleep, she thought about him, and the searching look on his face when he looked at her. Did she love him? She thought she might. Although, she still didn't think it would be fair to tell him that. If things couldn't work out for them, however, she hoped that Caleb would be spared having deep feelings for her.

She wouldn't want both of them to live their lives unhappily and with regrets about what could have been.

Caleb sat up and waited for his mother and sister to return home. It was almost ten thirty before headlights flashed in the uncurtained windows, announcing their arrival.

He headed out to the car to assist his mother.

"Caleb! I didn't mean for you to wait up for us."

"It was my pleasure to do so." It wasn't just a line that he said. Caleb's mother was the strongest person he knew. He loved her fiercely, and he had boundless respect for her. Regardless of how late they had planned to be out, he would always wait up for her. And he suspected that she knew that.

He paid the driver and assisted his family into the *haus*.

"I assume Miriam is already in bed," Rhoda stated, hanging her heavy black bonnet, the one she wore whenever she traveled, on the rack next to the door. She reached out and grabbed her mother's bonnet as well.

"I need to talk to you about that. Something happened. While you were gone, two men broke into the *haus*."

He didn't go into too much detail, but he related to them the story of how he, Miriam, and Ella Mae were all kidnapped at gunpoint. He glossed over the more horrifying details and focused on their escape, and the fact that Miriam and her daughter were now staying with her sister and that there was lots of police protection there.

His mother and sister exclaimed and were properly dismayed. They weren't afraid, though, that the men might *cumme* back and attack them. Their strong faith had carried them through much in the past few years.

Once he'd relayed the story, he returned to his room. Sleep eluded him for a long time. But it wasn't kidnappers and murderers that kept him awake. It was the look in Miriam's eyes as he said goodbye that evening. That look when she said she wanted to see him again.

It wasn't smart. He knew it wasn't smart. He was Amish. She had shown no hint that she planned on returning to the Amish lifestyle. So where did that leave them?

Nowhere. He could not leave his community. No matter how much he had grown to care for her, or how much he wanted Ella Mae to be his own little girl, it could never happen as long as she was still *Englisch*.

Why had he kissed her? It was a small kiss. Actually, it was barely a kiss. But he couldn't forget the taste of her lips. Nor could he stop wishing for more.

When Caleb woke Sunday morning his first thought was how Miriam had fared during the night. He told himself she was fine. Why wouldn't she be fine? There were people all around her, the police knew what was going on, and she was a smart woman. She would be careful and try to stay out of any dangerous situations.

Nothing he said worked. The worry festered in his heart.

He took care of the animals in record time. Since it was Sunday, only essential work, such as feeding the animals, would be done.

His mother and sister weren't in the kitchen yet. It was too early to go over to Gideon and Beth's *haus*. He knew it. Still, he looked at the clock and tried to figure out what time would be the earliest that he could respectfully show up at their *haus*.

Mamm wheeled into the kitchen. "You are done with feeding the animals early, *sohn*."

"*Ja*. As soon as breakfast is done, I'm going to take the buggy and drive to Gideon Bender's *haus*."

Mamm speared him with a concerned glance. They both knew it wasn't Gideon he was going to see.

"Guard your heart, Caleb," she warned him. "I like Miriam, too. But you know our two worlds don't mix. I want you to marry, and I want you to be happy. But this attraction you have for Miriam is not *gut*."

Caleb didn't wince but it was a near thing. "I know nothing will come of it while she is not Amish. She may never decide to become Amish. I will be smart. I will be careful."

More than that, he would not, could not, promise. If he said he wouldn't go over to Gideon's *haus* later, he might end up breaking his word, and Caleb never broke his word. Better to not make a promise then to say one that he couldn't keep.

She sighed, but didn't argue with him. Instead, she started gathering what she needed for a quick breakfast.

Caleb couldn't have even remembered what he ate for breakfast. When breakfast was done, he kissed his mother on the cheek and bolted from the *haus*. He brought the old mare in from the pasture and hooked her up to the buggy. Then he headed out to Gideon's *haus*.

Beth met him at the door. "Good morning, Caleb. Don't break my sister's heart."

What was this? Was every woman he met today going to tell him not to get involved with Miriam, or warn him about the dangers of breaking her heart? If it wasn't so annoying, he might find it amusing.

She led him into the kitchen. "Look who I found, sis."

Miriam was in the process of feeding Ella Mae. "Look, Ella Mae! Caleb is here."

Ella Mae waved her fists in the air. "Kay! Kay!"

Both Miriam and Caleb stared, jaws dropping. "Did she just say my name?"

Miriam nodded. "Uh-huh. That's her second word. I'm glad she said *Mama* first."

Although her tone was joking, her face spoke of her concern. Ella Mae was young. She probably didn't see him as a father figure. But again, he was reminded of the need to be circumspect. He couldn't be raising expectations and breaking women's hearts.

As soon as Ella Mae finished eating, Miriam cleaned her up.

"Um, do you think we can go for a walk? Talk for a few minutes?"

"Yes…"

Beth whisked up Ella Mae. "Go, I've got her. Just be back at lunch."

"Thanks." Miriam kissed her sister and her daughter. Then she grabbed a water bottle from the icebox. "Do you want one?"

He shook his head. "Let's go for a short buggy ride. I know a nice park we can walk. It's peaceful there."

They walked to the buggy, their bodies close enough that their hands touched several times. But they didn't hold hands. Caleb had to clench his hands a couple of times to avoid doing just that.

It was strange having her riding beside him on the bench rather than sitting in the back. It was almost like they were a couple. He could imagine such a thing. He tried to keep his mind on other things. It was difficult, though, with Miriam sitting close enough for him to smell the lemon scent she used in her hair.

At the park, she got down from the buggy without waiting for him to help her. Ah. She'd been warned, too.

They sat on the grass near the pond. He had a list of things he wanted to say, but suddenly, sitting beside her, his mind was a blank.

Then he heard a sharp crack. A blazing pain spread over his shoulder."

"Caleb!" she shrieked next to him. He felt a little dizzy. She helped him lie down before he fell.

"Hey," she yelled. "Call nine-one-one. Tell them someone's been shot."

Caleb opened his eyes. She was leaning over him, then it struck him. She was trying to protect him. "Go hide in the buggy. I'm fine."

"You come with me."

She helped him stand, and then she settled his arm across her shoulder. Together, they weaved their way to the buggy. He wasn't hurt that badly, he knew, but he was bleeding.

Once in the buggy, she removed her apron.

"What are you doing?"

"First aid." She grabbed her water bottle. Frowned. "I thought I'd closed this."

She offered it to him. "Not thirsty."

Taking her apron, she held it against his wound, pressing down to stem the flow.

When she began coughing, he waved his uninjured hand at the water bottle. "Go ahead and drink it."

She took a long sip of water. A couple ran to the buggy. "The ambulance will be here soon."

She thanked them. It was only a few minutes later when they heard the siren. The paramedics rushed to the buggy. He noticed they were the same paramedics that had come out to see her the first time.

"We have to stop meeting this way," one paramedic joked. The other scowled. Apparently, he didn't approve of dark humor.

The serious paramedic looked at Caleb's wound.

"You did well. It looks like most of the bleeding has stopped. Let's get him to the hospital and then the police will meet us there. You can follow along in the buggy."

Miriam shook her head. "Oh, no. Every time one of us looks the other way, someone gets hurt. I am riding in the back of that ambulance all the way to the hospital."

He wasn't exactly sure how it happened, but Miriam on a

rampage was a force to be reckoned with. The next thing he knew, he was sitting in the back of the ambulance, and she was sitting next to him holding his hand. He kept his eyes open, because frankly it was amusing to see the paramedic giving her exasperated looks every time she got in his way.

Once they were secure, the ambulance took off, sirens blasting. They were only a few minutes from the hospital. When they arrived, she let go of his hand long enough for him to be removed from the back of the ambulance and wheeled into the emergency room. Once there, she was back at his side and would not be displaced.

As happy as he was to have her there, one thought wouldn't leave his mind. The only reason they were at the hospital was because he didn't listen to what his conscience told him. If he had resisted the urge to see her this morning, he would not be sitting here in the hospital with a bullet wound. Another thought haunted him. Next time, it could be her with the bullet in her flesh.

And next time, it could be fatal.

He would not be responsible for another little girl growing up without her mother. He knew much of Miriam's pain and anguish had begun with her mother's death. When they left the hospital later, he would somehow find the strength to stay away from her. Her life might depend on it.

Caleb tried to smile. He'd enjoy this time he had now. Once he walked away from her, he wasn't sure what joy would be left in his life.

But she would be alive. And that precious little girl would grow up knowing her mother's love.

Caleb would be left with nothing but a single kiss, sweet memories, and a heart full of regrets.

FIFTEEN

Caleb winced when the emergency-room doctor cleaned his wound. Miriam moved around the equipment and sat next to him.

"How bad does it hurt?" She took his opposite hand in hers. When the doctor gave her the stink eye, she withdrew her hand. Or she tried to. Caleb held on with a vise grip. At least she still had use of one hand. She took a small sip of the water bottle she held.

"You're not leaving me," he whispered out of the side of his mouth.

The emergency-room doctor scoffed. Behind his thick-rimmed glasses, she thought she saw him roll his eyes. However, between the glasses and the bushy eyebrows that nearly eclipsed her view of his eyes, she wasn't positive.

"He's looking for sympathy. This isn't really that bad," the doctor commented. "The bullet barely grazed the skin. I know it bled a bit, but it should heal well."

"*Danke*, Darren." Caleb sighed, something in his voice telling her that the men were friends. Which was good. She couldn't imagine a doctor talking about a patient that way if they weren't friends.

"Will you have to use stitches?" Miriam asked, her lips quivering. She blinked. Her vision seemed a little fuzzy.

Taking a deep breath, she tried to clear her foggy thinking. Maybe she should take another drink of water. She made a face at the taste. She didn't remember bottled water being this bad.

"Not for this one." Darren motioned the nurse to come closer. "We'll use Steri-Strips for this wound."

Caleb squinted at him. "Steri what?"

"Steri-Strips." He held one up.

Caleb stared, incredulous. "You're going to tape my arm? After I've been shot?"

Miriam slapped a hand over her mouth, but a giggle escaped, anyway.

"I can use Steri-Strips, a needle, and sutures, or staples."

Caleb shuddered. "Tape me up. I do not want to see what a skin staple looks like."

She laughed. "Poor Caleb. I'm glad you'll be fine."

She took another sip of water. Enough. She could not drink this swill, no matter how thirsty she was. She set it on the table, then headed back to her chair. Moving became challenging. Her limbs were so heavy. Just a few more steps. She needed to move forward, but swayed. She had to stop in place.

"Miriam? What's wrong?"

She worked to focus her eyes on Caleb. "Nothing. The water tastes funny."

The room got blurry, grew dim.

Her face lost all color. She swayed on her feet. "Miriam!"

"I don't feel so good." She was so tired. She slumped. Started to slide.

She fell over. And everything went black.

"Miriam!" Caleb shouted, forgetting he was in the emergency room getting taped up. He hopped off the table and helped the nurse lift her onto the table he'd vacated.

"Caleb, stop!" the doctor exclaimed. "You can't jump around like that. I'd haven't finished taping up your injury. We will call in for another bed for her."

"I don't need my injury taped up anymore. I am quite well."

The doctor continued to protest. Both Caleb and the nurse ignored him.

"Do her lips look blue? I think her lips are blue." Caleb bounced on his feet. He waited for the nurse to complete checking Miriam's vitals. Why hadn't he noticed something was wrong with her? She'd seemed a bit emotional, more than normal. And sleepy. She'd been blinking and rubbing her eyes before she passed out.

She'd also been thirsty.

"She said the water tasted funny!"

The doctor moved quickly to her discarded water and smelled it. He furrowed his brow. "It has a funny smell. Not strong, but something…" He dabbed a finger in, then touched it to his tongue.

"Your girlfriend has been drugged. There's no doubt about it." He lifted her eyelids and flashed a light in her eyes. "Her pupils are small.

"Call the police in here. They were in the waiting room." The doctor listened to her heart and lungs while the nurse scurried to the nurse's station. "Her heart and lungs sound good. I don't know why anyone would drug someone at the hospital."

Caleb analyzed what he knew. She'd brought the water from home. He'd had water, too, and hadn't been affected, so it wasn't in the well. When would anyone have had a chance to drug her water?

Then he knew. The shooting.

Steve and Sergeant Yates rushed into the cubicle.

"It was a decoy!" Caleb yelled. "He shot me but I wasn't really the target. While I was being looked after, they drugged her water, knowing it would knock her out."

Steve's face shuttered. "They planned to kidnap Miriam. Now that Ella Mae is out of their reach. Who knows why they want her. It can't be good."

Caleb's mind continued to race, rejecting possibilities. How did he do this?

"I'm not sure if it's Owen McCallister or his cousins," he said. "They're all working together, we know that. If they shot me and drugged her, then one of them was probably supposed to grab her."

"Why didn't they?" Sergeant Yates asked.

Caleb laughed. It was an ugly, angry snarl of a laugh, devoid of humor. "They didn't grab Miriam because there were too many other people around. Even after the ambulance arrived, they couldn't grab her because she isn't who they thought she was. They expected some prissy little princess who would flee at the sight of blood and let the police handle everything. But she never gave them the chance to get to her."

Steve nodded. "That certainly is what they would have expected from Tim's wife. But Miriam changed and wasn't like that at all."

"I don't think she ever was. As a kid, she could be selfish and manipulative. But Miriam was never a coward."

"I'm not criticizing her. The important thing is, instead of making it easy to grab her, Miriam stuck right by your side."

"She did. She was the one who administered the first aid, and she didn't leave me even once the paramedics arrived. She made sure she was in the ambulance."

Steve thought for a long moment. "I need to look at all

the security footage, from the time you arrived at the hospital until now. After they drugged her, I don't think they would have left her. They would have followed to see if there was a chance to swipe her."

Which meant someone who wanted to kidnap Miriam was still on the hospital grounds. It was imperative that he get her out of the hospital as soon as she woke up. But where could he bring her so she would be safe?

Steve left his side and went over to talk with the doctor. A few moments later, he made eye contact with Sergeant Yates and exchanged a meaningful glance. The younger man nodded and stepped closer to Caleb and Miriam. Steve and the emergency room doctor left the cubicle together.

"What are they doing?"

Sergeant Yates shrugged, hesitancy clouding his features. "I may be wrong. But I believe they are going to search the security footage together."

Caleb's forehead furrowed. "Does the doctor know what they look like?"

Sergeant Yates shook his head. "He doesn't. But he would not give his permission without a warrant unless he could be right there to supervise the entire process."

There were too many rules to follow in the *Englisch* world. Even when someone was in trouble, they had to jump through hoops before they could lend a hand and help someone. That wasn't the way he wanted to live his life. There would never be any place for him in the *Englisch* world. No matter how much he cared for Miriam and her daughter, if there was any future for them, Miriam would have to be the one to leave everything she knew behind.

Would she be willing to do that?

That was a problem that needed to wait. Right now, Miriam and Ella Mae were in danger. He had promised her he'd stay with her and keep watch over her. It was time to put that promise into practice.

He sat down beside Miriam's bed, a prayer on his lips, while the woman he cherished slept off the drug.

It was dark out by the time Miriam woke. How did that happen? Why was she the one in a hospital bed?

Caleb sat in a chair on the left side of the narrow hospital bed, his eyes closed. When she shifted her gaze, she saw Steve on the right side, tapping on his phone. Sergeant Yates had taken up another chair against the wall.

She frowned. She was no longer in the waiting room. She'd been moved to a real room. An IV was hooked up, dripping fluids into the veins on the back on her hand.

She bolted upright. "Ella Mae!"

Caleb and both officers shot out of their seats. When they realized there was no immediate danger, all three resumed their previous positions. Caleb scooted his chair a little closer to the bed, then reached out and took her hand in his. When he leaned his forehead against their clasped hands, she realized how badly she had scared him.

Well, she was scared, too. She still didn't know what happened, or if her daughter was in danger. She cast a pleading glance at Steve. "Please. Tell me what happened. Why am I in a hospital bed? The last I remember Caleb was the one who got shot."

Steve ran a hand through his hair. His face looked haggard compared to the last time she'd seen him. "You've been asleep now for almost six hours."

"Six hours!" She was horrified. "How did this happen?"

Steve and Caleb took turns explaining the events. When she realized that someone had shot Caleb just so they could drug her and kidnap her, guilt exploded like dynamite in her soul.

"Caleb—"

"Don't say it." He squeezed her hand. "I've said it before. This was not your doing. Everyone makes their own choices, ain't so? Some choices are better than others."

Steve cleared his throat. "He's right, Miriam. This is nothing you should ever feel bad about. But I do have some news."

She clenched her hand, squeezing Caleb's fingers. "I'm ready. Hit me with it."

She knew without looking that Caleb probably rolled his eyes at her. He was not a fan of colloquialisms.

"After you climbed into the ambulance and came to the hospital with Caleb—by the way, your stubbornness probably saved your life—"

"I'll keep that in mind."

"As I was saying, the surgical director and I looked over the video footage from the time you were brought into the hospital until right after you collapsed. Owen McCallister's cousins, the ones who staged his prison break, followed the ambulance to the hospital. Most likely, their goal was to find you alone and bring you to Owen."

"They're here?" She trembled from head to foot.

Sergeant Yates broke in, a smug smirk on his youthful face. "They were here. Once we knew they were on the hospital grounds, they were surrounded and arrested. They are sitting in a jail cell right now waiting to be arraigned."

"And Owen McCallister?"

"He's still at large." Steve leaned toward her. "Your baby is safe at your sister's house. I sent my brother-in-law, Isaiah, out there to stay with them for the night. He brought his whole family. And when Micah, my other brother-in-law, got wind of it, he did the same. That little girl has six adults, two of whom worked in law enforcement for years, all there to watch over her. She won't be alone for a single second."

Relief rolled over her in waves. Her daughter would be fine.

"Thank you. I can't tell you how much better I feel knowing she's being watched over."

"I understand. I have children myself. I would do pretty much anything to keep them and my wife out of harm."

She nodded. "It's the middle of the night. I'm not tired at all. But I know you guys have to get some sleep. Since I'll be awake for a while, if you don't want to hang out, that's fine with me."

Caleb shook his head. "I'm not going anywhere. Even if I end up dozing off next to you, I'd still like to be here if you need me."

Steve stood and stretched. "I'm not going to leave, but now that you're awake I think Allen and I can take turns watching the door."

Sergeant Yates stood. "That sounds like a great plan. Shall I watch the waiting room first?"

"Fine." He suddenly recalled the instructions he'd received from Joss. "Oh, when she heard I'd be here, and that you were stuck here for the night, Joss sent this for you."

He opened his backpack and took out a well-worn copy of *Pride and Prejudice*. Followed by a small Bible. "She felt you would appreciate having these to read."

"Oh, yes! *Pride and Prejudice* is my favorite book!"

"She knows. Beth had told her that you used to borrow that book from the public library and renew it two or three times in a row."

The two officers left the room.

Miriam's face warmed. She hadn't realized Beth knew

her so well. She had wasted so much time in her youth. It shamed her to know how foolish she'd been.

"God uses it for good."

"Huh?" Caleb blinked at her, his expression adorably puzzled.

She smiled at Caleb. "I was thinking of how I'd wasted so much time, done so many foolish things. But then I remember the story of Joseph. When his brothers sold him into slavery, and years later, they were scared of his retribution. But he told them, 'But as for you, ye thought evil against me, *but* God meant it unto good…'"

"That's one of my favorite verses."

She smiled. "Mine, too. I remind myself of it that God is still in control, even when we chose wrong."

He picked up the novel and made a face. Then he opened the book, turned to chapter one, and began to read.

She grinned and snuggled onto her side so she could watch him as he read to her.

The next morning, the doctor released her from the hospital. She and Caleb journeyed with Steve to Beth's house. When they arrived, Beth met them outside with Ella Mae.

When the child saw her mother, she wiggled in Beth's arms and held out hers to Miriam. "Mama, mama."

Overjoyed, Miriam gathered her little one close and breathed in her soft baby scent.

A whole crowd of people gathered round. She felt a little intimidated, but then a line from *Pride and Prejudice* ran through her mind, one about how Elizabeth's courage rose with every attempt to intimidate her. So, fortified, she grinned and met her sister's extended family.

It was Caleb's family, too, she realized.

And hers. Because of Beth.

It felt good having people around.

SIXTEEN

Caleb watched Miriam interact with her sister and her family. She seemed so happy. This was how it could be. If she would leave her world and join his.

At first, it felt hopeless. But seeing her now, smiling and laughing, confident and comfortable in her Amish dress and *kapp*, he had to wonder if it was so ridiculous. She remembered the Pennsylvania Dutch sprinkled in with the *Englisch* words. And though she tended to speak *Englisch*, the faith she espoused aligned with the *Ordnung*.

As lunchtime approached, Micah, Steve, and Isaiah took their families home. Sergeant Yates remained. Another officer, Lieutenant Kathy Bartlett, would be out to help keep watch when she finished an interview at the station.

There was no reason for him to remain.

No reason other than the woman he loved, and the *kind* he adored as if she was his own, remained here.

Last night, while he read to her, she'd kept her hand in his. She eventually had fallen asleep. He'd put down the book and watched over her. Now, he was so tired his eyes burned. It didn't matter. He would not trade a minute he'd spent in her presence.

But now what?

As soon as they caught Owen McCallister, what would

happen? Would she go back home? Indeed, he'd heard her talking with Steve and Sergeant Yates. They had told her they could set up some kind of protective detail plan with the precinct where she lived.

They also offered to talk with Micah about witness protection, as Micah was a deputy US Marshal.

His heart was breaking apart in his chest as he thought about it. She would go back to the *Englisch* world and he would lose her forever.

It wasn't fair. He'd finally met a woman who made his heart throb in his chest and who took his breath away.

And he was going to lose her.

There was no way he could follow her if she left for the *Englisch* world. His soul would shrivel and die in that environment. This was where *Gott* had placed him.

"Caleb!" Miriam's breezy voice carried a happy lilt as she approached.

He squeezed his eyes shut.

"Caleb?" She was at his side. He opened his eyes and gazed at her loveliness. She still wore the *kapp* and the purple dress she'd borrowed. She looked Amish. What was she in her heart?

"I've been looking for you." She smiled. "Do you like my family? It was only Beth and I growing up. Now, I have so many brothers and sisters. It's unbelievable."

"Will you keep in touch with them?" He really meant, are you leaving them, too.

She tilted her head and regarded him. "I'm not sure what you're really trying to say. I want them in my life, yes. And I want Ella Mae to grow up and know them and all her cousins. She's going to have a lot of them."

Her blue eyes rolled at her joke. He didn't smile. How

did one find joy when their person was a minute from saying goodbye?

"Hey." Her warm hand touched his. "I can see something's wrong. What's bothering you?"

Suddenly, he grew angry. "It's you."

The joy left her face. It closed down. "I don't understand."

He was doing this all wrong. But he could not stop. "You will leave us, and then what? I heard you talking with Steve. Making plans to go home. Do I mean nothing to you?"

She went pale. "You know you do. You and Ella Mae are the most important people in my life."

"Then why go back?"

"I don't want to. But I also have obligations I need to take care of. Things I need to do. And I can't expect a small force like Sutter Springs to sleep at my sister's house until the bad guy is caught. Nor can I keep putting them in harm's way." Her voice softened. "Look, we can still see each other. Visit each other. And then when he's caught, everything will change."

He knew what she was saying, but it hurt so much, losing her. He didn't know if he was strong enough. "What if he's never caught?"

She put her hand to her throat.

"You'll put us on hold forever, meaning we'll always be waiting and hoping. I don't know if I can do that. I spent three years in a coma. I don't want to spend the rest of my life waiting."

She stepped toward him, stopping when he backed away. "Caleb, what are you saying?"

"I'm sorry, Miriam. I can't accept this. There is no us. If you are staying in the *Englisch* world, whatever is growing between us is over."

He turned and stomped away from her. Climbing into his buggy, he didn't look back as he steered the mare onto the road and kicked her into a trot at the first possible instant.

He didn't know how he'd ever get over her.

What just happened?

Miriam wiped her sleeve across her face, absorbing the tears she didn't want her sister to see. How had she read the situation so wrong? Last night, they'd been so easy together. He'd sat with her, his voice warm and soothing with that little bit of grit that made her shiver. He'd read to her from a book that he was not enjoying, yet he did so because the story brought her joy.

Then today, she'd met family she'd never dreamed she had and been accepted. And it had nothing to do with what she wore. Micah, Isaiah, and Joss all left the Amish community, and they were well-loved, as were their spouses and children.

But they married non-Amish people.

That was the difference. As much as his words angered her, she understood, to a point. She had pretty much asked him to wait for her indefinitely because she might one day be available to be with him.

What man wanted to hear that?

What if they never caught Owen McCallister? She shuddered at the thought. She had asked for a huge leap of faith from Caleb.

More than that, she hadn't even said she wanted to be Amish. She knew he had joined the Amish church. In order for him to leave, he'd lose all connection with his mother and his sisters. She could not do that to him.

"Miriam!" She turned to see Beth waving at her. Ella Mae fussed in her arms, rubbing her eyes. "I think your *boppli* is ready for a nap."

She went to her sister and gathered Ella Mae close. "I think you're right. I'll put her down."

She left her sister there, not yet wanting to divulge her thoughts. They were still too raw. She heard Sergeant Yates on the phone. The other officer hadn't arrived yet. They hadn't known what time to expect her, anyway.

Would Caleb truly stay away until after she'd left?

She'd come so close to saying she loved him, but knew she could not do that to him. The words had been on her tongue, but it had been too soon. Plus, she knew it wouldn't be fair. But she'd still hurt him. Just like she had hurt Gideon so many years before. Gideon had at least found Beth. Would Caleb move on?

Her gut clenched. She didn't want him to move on. He belonged with her.

Except he didn't. Not while they still had their feet planted in different cultures.

Ella Mae fretted, making it difficult to put her down for her nap. Miriam gathered a soft blanket and sat in the handmade rocking chair next to the crib. As she sang to her daughter, rocking her to sleep, silent tears rolled down her face and dripped onto the blanket. Finally, the baby drifted off. Miriam kissed her temple and lay her daughter down in the crib.

She wanted to stay in the room and sulk. However, she was no longer a child or a spoiled teenager. She was a woman, a mother, and she had responsibilities that she needed to own up to.

She made her way back downstairs. Beth wasn't in the house. She went out the front door and walked around until she found Beth in the backyard hanging laundry.

"What can I do to help?" Whenever she felt sad or angry, having something to occupy herself helped her. Otherwise, she tended to brood, and dwell over things that she had no control over. Because as much as she wanted to change his mind, Caleb was a grown man and had a right to his own opinion and feelings.

"*Ja*, you can help." Beth gave her a wide smile. Miriam had a feeling that Beth could tell she was out of sorts. But her sister was a rare woman. She would not prod her for information but would wait until Miriam was ready to talk. She had never truly appreciated her sister's kind and sensitive nature. She appreciated it now.

"Great! What do you need?"

"I'm fixing potato salad to have with dinner tonight. And I have not started to peel and dice the potatoes."

"Sure. I can do that. How many do you want done?"

"The whole bag. I think we will have a house full again tonight. I don't mind. Having family around is always a pleasure, ain't so?"

Miriam shrugged. She didn't have much experience with that. "I guess. Last night was the first time I've ever seen a full house like that. Remember, growing up it was just you, me, and *daed*. We rarely went to visit out-of-state relatives. And I didn't get to know the family you married into until now."

"A big family is fun. You will see!"

"I'll take your word for it. I'll grab those potatoes."

"Miriam…"

She pivoted and walked backward a few steps. "Yeah?"

"If you want to talk…"

Miriam was tempted to tell her sister she was fine and guard all the hurt building up inside. Then she stopped. She'd kept her sister out of her life for too long. Glancing back at Beth, she saw the hopeful gleam in her eye.

"Actually, I would like to talk. If you have a few minutes."

"For family, anything."

She didn't tell her sister everything. Some things, such as her growing feelings for Caleb, still needed to be sorted out. She did tell her about her first marriage, and Owen McCallister.

Even though she tried to keep some things back, Beth seemed to hear things she hadn't said. When she stood to go get the potatoes, Beth called out, "I'll listen if you want to talk about Caleb, too, you know."

At that moment, love for her younger sister crashed over her. She embraced her, hard.

"I'm not ready yet. When I am, you're the first person I'll go to. Promise." It surprised her how much she meant those words. There was a time when she disdained her little sister and did everything she could to disturb her peace. Now, she almost envied her.

After picking up the five-pound sack of potatoes her sister had set on the counter, she carried it and a bucket to the front porch. She tucked her skirt demurely around her legs, then sat on the top step and began to peel the potatoes. Peeling the potatoes was a good task for her current mood. It didn't take much thought, so she could not mess it up, and it took a bit of repetitive physical motion to help rid some of the tension and anguish.

Should she try to see Caleb again before she left? Would it do any good? Or maybe she should leave things as they were. If she saw him, it might make things worse.

Although, at this point, he'd basically severed ties with her. How much worse could it get?

A hard object pressed against her temple. She froze, the knife falling from her hands.

"They finally left you alone." Owen McCallister stood over her, a gun held to her head. "Where's your little girl, Miriam?"

Whatever reason he had for wanting to know where Ella Mae was, she wasn't about to cooperate and let him near her baby. Not today. "She's in the custody of the police."

He glanced at the cruiser sitting in the yard. A scowl flitted across his bold features. Then he shrugged. "I'll deal with her later. But you are coming with me."

He put the gun in the waistband of his jeans and yanked her to her feet. The potatoes went everywhere. Grabbing her wrists hard, he dragged her across the yard. She screamed.

Whirling, he backhanded her. She tasted blood. His eyes were wild as he searched the surroundings. "Do that again and I won't care who I kill."

Before she could gather her breath, he slung her over his shoulder and took off running. The force of her abdomen bouncing on his hard shoulder knocked the breath out of her, destroying any ability to scream or cry for help.

"Miriam! Where are you?" Beth cried from the yard.

She could not answer.

She feared that when they found her, if they found her, it would be too late for her.

SEVENTEEN

He'd been a fool to make demands on her.

That wasn't how you treated someone you loved. Shame filled Caleb.

Miriam had retreated to Beth and Gideon's *haus* to talk with her sister. He had no idea how long she planned to stay there. Maybe if he hurried, she'd agree to talk with him. Talking would entail him apologizing and begging her forgiveness.

He was willing to do that. Even if she never joined the Amish community, he didn't want to force her to make a choice. That wasn't up to him.

Nor did he want her to go not knowing how he felt about her.

That he loved her.

When he got to the *haus*, something wasn't right. Beth and Gideon stood outside, and a police cruiser was parked in their driveway, lights flashing. Nausea roiled within him as he eyed Steve and Sergeant Yates. They would not show up unless something was wrong. Although, hope sparked when he recalled that Steve was married to Joss, Gideon's twin sister.

The hope died when he looked at their faces. He pulled on the reins, bringing the mare to a full stop, then jumped down off his buggy and rushed toward the small group assembled on the front lawn. His feet felt like he was running in the sand, churning it beneath his weight. He'd had dreams before where he was running and getting nowhere. Now, he experienced it in real life.

"Beth!" he shouted when he was almost to them. "Gideon! Where is Miriam?"

Beth turned toward him, and his heart shattered in his chest. Tear tracks stained her cheeks, and redness rimmed her eyes.

Oh, no.

"Is she alive?"

Beth nodded. "I think so. I have to believe she is. But he has her. That man, the one who killed her husband, he has her."

Her head dropped into her hands. Fresh weeping burst from her.

Steve put his hand on her shoulder while Gideon wrapped his arm around his wife's waist. Caleb rocked on his feet. He could not lose her. Not now. Even if they could not be together, a world without Miriam seemed a terrible place.

Steve patted her shoulder. "Beth, you know I'm not doubting your word, but I need to know. Are you sure it was Owen McAllister who took her? Is it possible your sister decided to return to her old life without telling you?"

Once it might have been a valid question. True, Miriam had taken off years ago, but that wasn't who she was anymore. Miriam was responsible and loving, and she'd never abandon her daughter. Never. Hot anger filled his chest. Caleb opened his mouth to argue. Steve lifted a hand to silence him before he spoke a word.

"I'm not criticizing Miriam. But we need to have all the

facts to find her as soon as possible. Our feelings, while I know they are valid, are not what will help her."

Beth sniffed. "I understand. We were talking and she told me all about what happened with——" Her eyes cut to Caleb.

He could see her revising her statement in her head. "Say it, Beth. I know about her husband. Don't worry about me."

She nodded. "We were talking about what happened to Tim, her husband. She showed me the picture that she brought from the police station. The one from the database with his picture. The man who killed Tim and Dina. I'm sure he's the one who took her. Who else could it be? The picture's still in the *haus*. I know what that evil man looks like."

She wiped her face with her apron. Steve and Gideon made encouraging noises, and Gideon's face pinched across his cheekbones. Caleb felt for him. It had to be hard listening to your wife talk, knowing her heart was breaking, and be unable to help her.

Beth took a deep breath and continued. "I was hanging up the laundry in the backyard. Ella Mae was in the upstairs bedroom taking a nap. Miriam had gone to sit on the front porch and peel the potatoes for dinner."

From where he stood, Caleb saw the basket of potatoes flipped over in the dirt, peeled skins scattered over the steps. His mouth dried like he'd been chewing on cotton balls.

"Then what happened?" Steve urged.

"I heard Miriam yell. It wasn't an angry yell. It was a scared one. Terrified. I ran to the front. I saw him dragging her away through the woods. I tried to chase after her."

She broke down again. No one asked her why she didn't follow. Even though the Amish don't talk about pregnancy, it was obvious that Beth was with child. She could not run fast.

"It's okay, Mrs. Bender," Sergeant Yates added, speaking for the first time. "You did nothing wrong."

Beth straightened. "I went to the barn and I used the business phone to call you, Steve. Then I called Gideon."

"You did well, Beth. We've already circulated his image and the image from Miriam's driver's license. People are looking for them. We've got a BOLO out. We will do everything we can to find her."

Caleb looked at Beth, sympathy twisting his heart. "You said Ella Mae is safe?"

She nodded. "I just checked on her—she's still asleep but she's going to wake up soon. I need to be there when she does."

Steve and Sergeant Yates began to make their way back to the police cruiser. Caleb rushed after them. He could not sit here and do nothing while they were off searching for the woman he loved.

"Steve! Wait for me!"

Steve slowed and rotated to face him, eyebrows nearly hidden beneath his hairline. Caleb strode to stand before him.

"I'm coming with you." He wasn't asking. If his mother had been there, she'd probably tell him he had his stubborn face on. That was fine with him. He would be belligerent and argumentative if it helped. Caleb Schultz was done letting others rescue his girl.

Even if she wasn't really.

Sergeant Yates opened his mouth, most likely to tell him "Not on your life." Steve, however, gave Caleb a long look of understanding before he waved him on.

"Come on. You'll have to sit in the back."

Sergeant Yates's eyes bulged to the point that Caleb half expected them to fall clean out of his head.

He didn't give them a chance to change their minds. Nor did he care where he sat as long as he was able to go along and be part of the search for Miriam. It was probably forty-five minutes when they got a lead.

The dispatcher called them. Steve answered the phone on speaker. "A green truck was spotted heading down Lake Hill Road toward Heller Park. The caller said the man driving looked like Owen McCallister."

"Did she see Miriam Troyer?"

"No, Lieutenant Beck. She did say the truck had a cap on over the bed."

Sergeant Yates glanced back at Caleb. "There was no cap before."

Was this a good sign?

"She may be stowed in the truck bed. Have the drones fly over that road. Let me know when you have something."

Caleb stared out the window, watching the scenery flash by. They were headed in the right direction, he hoped. But would they arrive in time. Leaning his forehead against the cool glass, he prayed for Miriam's safe return.

When the dispatcher called back, he sat forward to hear the call. When he heard her say the drone spotted the truck in the lot of an old, abandoned farmhouse, chills and anticipation raced up his spine.

"On the way. Please send backup and an ambulance. Tell them to go in silent mode and wait for my directions. A life is at stake here."

Breathing deeply to calm his racing nerves, Caleb sat back.

We're coming, Miriam. Hold on.

Miriam struggled to escape Owen's clutches, desperate to get back to her daughter. She was no match for his strength.

He'd dragged her along the dirt path, his hands hurting her. Branches scraped against her arms, face, and neck. Any place not covered by her dress or *kapp*. And still, he pulled her along as if she weighed no more than Ella Mae.

She sobbed, begging him to let her go. She attempted to use her heels to halt their forward momentum. It didn't work. Instead of slowing him down, all she managed to do was kick up dust. She tripped over a root and fell forward.

Owen yanked her arms, forcing her to her feet again.

"Stand up," he growled at her. "If you don't want your daughter to suffer in your place."

Miriam thought her heart stopped beating. Then it took off, beating wildly. She would do anything for her baby girl. Even if that meant dying.

She wasn't done fighting, though. If there was a way, God would get her out of this. Her heart called out for Caleb.

It was too late. He'd walked away from her, knowing that as long as she was not Amish, there was no future for them.

Was this really the world she wanted to belong to? The culture she wanted her daughter raised in? Suddenly, she realized in running from the Amish, she truly had been the creator of her own misery. Her own discontent was responsible for her present situation. If she could go back and change her decisions...

But then she would not have Ella Mae. And she could never regret that precious life.

Her thoughts stuttered to a halt when they arrived at that green truck. The color itself stood out like some malevolent beacon. Her struggles increased. If he got her in the truck, her opportunity to escape would be over.

He held her wrists in a bruising grip. She cried out, positive he'd crushed the bones. He grabbed a rope from the bed of the truck and looped it around her hands, binding them together with a tight square knot. Then he lifted her from the ground and tossed her into the bed of the truck. She crashed into the back wall.

He laughed. "You go ahead and cry all you want. Ain't nobody out here going to hear you anymore."

He slammed the tailgate up and securely latched the truck cap, enclosing her in the silence. The vehicle rocked slightly. He hopped into the front seat. The engine roared to life like some ancient dinosaur from a horror movie she'd watched the year before. Inside the truck, the radio was cranked up and rock music blared loudly.

No wonder he didn't care if she cried. No one would be able to hear her over that music. Hot tears slid down her face, dripping onto the floor of the truck bed.

What would she do now? She had no hope. Except...

Why was she still alive? He could have easily killed her in the woods instead of dragging her to his truck. He'd killed Dina. He'd tried to kill her before. Why was she still alive?

Not that she minded. Being alive meant she still had a chance.

She lost track of time. When the truck finally rumbled to a stop, the right side of her body was numb from lying on her side while the moving vehicle vibrated beneath her.

She had no time to prepare for his reappearance when he opened the tailgate and lifted her from her prison. Owen threw her over his shoulder and carried her like she was a bag of potatoes. Her flopped her down on a metal folding chair in the middle of what looked like a tool shed. Dusty cobwebs hung in thick strings all along the ceiling, draping down and nearly touching his head.

"I bet you're wondering why you ain't dead yet," he said. The smile he leveled at her was oddly gentle. It was creepier than if he had growled and snarled at her. This friendly, charming demeanor shook her more than his anger had. "Your husband and I were 'business partners,' I guess you could say." He held up his hands and made air quotes. The rather juvenile gesture wasn't amusing. "However, my partner stole from me. I sold the merchandise, and he delivered it. That was out agreement. He didn't think I'd notice that he was taking a share of the drugs I'd already sold and selling on the it on the side so he could make more money. After I killed him, my clients demanded either their product or their money back."

Miriam swallowed the bile that rose, burning her throat. She'd had no idea this was going on.

"I've been watching you for a while. You don't spend money the way a woman with access to five million dollars spends."

She gasped, unable to hold it back. "I don't know anything about it. I don't have five million dollars!"

He laughed in her face. "Oh, I believe you. You may not have known about the money, but your husband definitely had it. I need to know where it is. I was searching your apartment when your roommate came home. Shame. I never intended for her to die."

His cold eyes held no remorse for Dina's death. In fact, she thought he enjoyed killing.

"I didn't plan for you to die that day, but you'd seen my face again. I thought maybe we could come to an agreement. You give me the money, and I leave your daughter alone."

"I don't know where the money is!"

He smirked. Her blood froze. He knew she didn't know where the money was. "I need to move on to plan B."

She shuddered at the look in his eyes. "Plan B?"

"Yeah. If you can't give me the money, then I have a buyer who will gladly take your daughter for a nice price."

Heat pumped through her veins. He wanted her to tell him where the money was, then he'd kill her and still go after her little girl. There was no way this man was getting his hands on Ella Mae.

He started walking toward her. His hand reached back into the waistband of his jeans. He was going for his gun. She could not let him get to it. If he did, both she and Ella Mae were dead.

"This is your last chance."

Fear gave her strength she didn't know she possessed. Miriam leaped out of her chair and grabbed one side with her bound hands. She whipped it across at him, striking him in the knees. He yelled and stumbled to the ground. She turned the door. Before she could reach it, he latched on to her ankle. She snatched a can of wasp killer from the shelf against the wall and whirled around, yanking her ankle from his grip. She took a step back, aimed the bottle, and hit the nozzle. The spray hissed and squirted from the nozzle, hitting Owen in the face.

A blood-curdling scream of agony shot from him. Owen dropped and rolled on the floor, his clawed hands digging at his eyes.

The toolshed door whipped open behind her. Miriam turned and stumbled right into Caleb's arms. They curved around her, holding her close while she sobbed out her fear and anger on his warm shoulder.

He'd found her.

Caleb sent up a prayer of thanksgiving. She was safe. He repeated the words again and again.

"Yes, I'm safe."

He hadn't realized he'd been saying it out loud.

"Are you hurt?" He gently steered her away from the shed entrance. The ambulance had arrived. Paramedics and the police had all congregated around Owen. Caleb could not care less about the state he was in.

"I'm okay. Bruised. Angry. But he didn't hurt me."

"Did you find out anything?" Steve asked, joining them. "Backup arrived. They will escort him to the hospital. Sergeant Yates will ride in the back of the ambulance, and a police car will lead the way. Another will follow behind. It's all hands on deck with this one."

She shuddered, huddling closer into Caleb's embrace. "The man is a monster."

She explained about him killing her husband because he'd been stealing and reselling drugs and keeping the profits.

When he heard how much money Tim had accumulated, he shook his head. "All this for money?"

"I know. It's worse, though. When I could not tell him anything, he told me he'd made a deal with someone to buy Ella Mae."

Both men exclaimed. Steve whipped out his phone. "I need to call this in. If there is child kidnapping and selling, we need to find those involved, fast."

"How will you do that?" she asked Steve, still not moving from Caleb's arms.

He wondered if she was even aware how hard she was clutching on to him. He didn't care. If she needed to hold on to him to steady herself, he was glad to be there for her. It would still hurt when, or if, she left. But he would remain faithful.

Caleb didn't think he'd ever be able to love another in his whole life. So if she did decide to remain in the *Englisch* world, he doubted he'd marry. Because while it would be nice to have a wife and raise a large family, or at least have a few *kinder*, it would not be fair to any woman to pledge himself to her, knowing his heart belonged to another.

Nor did he think *Gott* would approve.

"We have him in custody," Steve told her. "We know he's murdered two people since he escaped prison. Not including the prison guards his cousins murdered. Knowing the additional threats, it won't be difficult to get a warrant to check his phone, his cousins' premises, all their accounts. At this point, if it's out there, I'm pretty sure we can get what we need to find it."

"Lieutenant Beck!" Steve waved at one of the other officers. "I got to go talk with them. Listen, I will be back in a few minutes. As soon as McCallister is contained, one of the paramedics will be over."

He sauntered away, leaving them alone.

"I don't want to see the paramedics," Miriam complained, a hint of desperation in her voice. "I want to go back to my sister's house. I need to see my daughter."

"*Ja*, I know you do. Steve will be back and he'll take us there."

She turned to face him. "I'm glad you're here. But why are you?"

He cupped her face with his hand. "I'm here because I love you."

Her eyes flared wide open. "You do?"

He nodded. "*Ja*. I do. I am sorry I argued with you yesterday. I didn't mean what I said. You have to make your own decisions. It wasn't my intent to rush you or make your decisions for you."

She placed her hand over his mouth, stopping his words. Unable to resist, he kissed her fingertips, grinning when she flushed. "You didn't force my hand. I've been think-ing of what you said. I love you, too. And I am not happy about returning to the *Englisch* world."

She gave him a look when he started to talk. "Let me fin-ish." He nodded, his heart in his throat. "Caleb, I do want to return to the Amish world. But I'm not sure now is the time. I have some things I need to finish. I need to do right by Dina."

He didn't know what that meant.

"I have some financial things to take care of. And I need to know, really know, that the threat is gone and I am safe to live my life where I want to."

His heart dropped to his feet.

Tears blurred his vision. His wiped his eyes. If today was the end of them, he wanted to see her clearly. "You're still leaving?"

"I have to." She squeezed his hands. "I'm not leaving forever. I plan on coming back. It's not fair for me to ask this. But I need to know. Will you still want me? Whenever I'm free to return?"

Hope lit his soul like a fuse. He bent and gently kissed her. "I will wait for you. Even if you're gone a year. Or lon-ger. I will be here waiting for you when you return."

After Steve dropped them off at Beth's *haus* and he drove home, he pondered the commitment he'd made.

He meant it with his whole being. He would wait for her to return. He didn't know how he'd get through every day, wondering when she'd return, but he'd put his trust in *Gott* and strive to be patient.

It was the only thing his love had asked of him.

EIGHTEEN

The first day Miriam walked out her apartment door wearing her sister's *kapp* and a long blue dress, she encountered stares from every tenant she passed. When they saw Ella Mae dressed in an adorable Amish dress and a little black *kapp*, their mouths invariably hit the floor.

One of her neighbors even asked her, confusion plastered on her face, if Miriam was headed to a costume party. Miriam bit back a sarcastic laugh. It was ten in the morning. Not exactly time for a party.

She recalled her decision to meet all with kindness, and merely smiled. The woman had no way of knowing that Miriam had grown up in an Amish community. She'd rarely talked to any of her neighbors. Dina had been the social one.

"No. I'm going to be returning home soon."

She left it at that, leaving her neighbor more confused than ever.

Steve called her two days after she arrived home. "We found the money. We'll have to take what was gotten illegally. Apparently, your husband loved to gamble. He had his winnings in a separate account. That's yours." She didn't want it, and told him so. "Well, that's your choice. You should also know that Owen is at the maximum-level security prison. He's never getting out. And the man he'd tried to sell your daughter to was found. He's also going away. You and your daughter are safe."

She cried when she heard that. Tears of relief. No more looking over her shoulder. No more guilt. Now, she had plans to make.

Her late husband had died a wealthy man. She'd used it to survive when she'd run the first time. Now, however, she wanted nothing to do with the tainted money. She paid all her bills and donated the rest of his money to charities for drug rehabilitation. Maybe it could be used to help someone.

Sergeant Yates had called the storage business and told them to expect her. Miriam had gone in and collected her things. She prayed about what to do about all her possessions. She had accumulated so much stuff. She recalled Caleb's house, and how pleasant and homey it had been without all the extra trappings.

She needed to get rid of it all.

What about her clothes? Should she keep those, just in case going home didn't work out? No. She needed to trust. She'd sell it all.

Between online selling, consignment shops, and thrift stores, she either sold or gave away almost everything of value. Including her wedding rings and the jewelry Tim had given her.

She would not save it for her daughter. Ella Mae would not grow up knowing the *Englisch* world. Maybe one day she'd choose it, like Miriam had, but Miriam would not give her anything that might encourage that choice.

Once she had sold everything, she took the checks to the bank. In the car, she leaned her head back against the seat. Caleb's image floated before her eyes. They stung. She held back the tears, but it was close. She didn't want to walk into the bank looking like she'd been weeping.

"Soon, Caleb. I'll come back to you soon."

Her heart ached every day thinking about him. Her treacherous mind warned her he might forget her, that she'd been gone so long. "He won't forget me. He loves me. I trust him."

Still, being separated from him hurt more than she'd ever imagined. But she had to do this right. And she could not return to him until she knew she could return to the Amish community. She'd never ask him to risk being shunned to come and live in her world.

Before she returned, though, there were a few more things to accomplish.

Resolved, she gathered Ella Mae and walked into the bank. An hour later, she walked out, stunned. She hadn't been keeping track of all the online payments going directly to her bank account. When she walked out, she felt slightly wobbly. In her purse, she had a cashier's check for fifteen thousand dollars, most of it from selling her jewelry. In addition, she had a hefty roll of cash in her purse so she could live independently until she joined the church and was baptized.

She didn't head back to her apartment. Instead, she drove east another hour until she arrived at a middle-class suburb. She followed her GPS to a comfortable one-story house in a quiet neighborhood.

Dina's parents weren't rich. They'd both worked hard and had raised three daughters. Dina told Miriam they'd spent thousands putting all three girls through college. When she decided to return and get her teaching degree, they'd been sad that they weren't able to help her out more.

They were still paying for her funeral.

She took Ella Mae out of the car and walked up the path to the house. She didn't know how Dina's parents would react to her presence. She hadn't been at the funeral. Dina's sister, Pam, had watched a news story about her disappearance. And later, when Owen had been arrested, she'd called Miriam to talk.

She'd been kind, but it was a hard phone call. They'd both cried. Pam had told her that none of the family held Miriam responsible, but until she talked to Dina's mom and dad, she'd never know for sure.

She knocked on the door and waited, bouncing Ella Mae on her hip when the little girl began to fuss. "I know, sweetie. You want down. I need you to be patient a few more minutes."

When she heard footsteps, she shifted her stance. Moments later, Dina's mom blinked at her. No doubt confused by the way Miriam was dressed. Within minutes, she sat across the table from Dina's parents. Both had choked back tears when they saw her, but neither had blamed her.

She'd had a long time to consider what she would say to them. She didn't want them to think she was giving them charity, nor did she want them to think of her gift as blood money.

"I don't know if Dina told this, but I grew up in an Amish community." She accepted a glass of ice water from Dina's mom. Ella Mae happily played in a bouncy standing toy.

Dina's mom, Patty, smiled sadly at the baby. "I keep that around for my grandchildren." She turned her attention back to Miriam. "She did mention that you'd once been Amish, yes."

Hal, Dina's dad, nodded his agreement.

"Well, I've been rethinking my life, and I have decided to return to the Amish community."

"I wondered when I saw you in the dress and bonnet."

Miriam didn't correct her. "I sold all my jewelry and

clothes. Things I won't need when I'm there. I kept what I needed, but I wanted to do something to honor Dina." She pulled the cashier's check from her purse. "I wanted to help with any expenses from the funeral."

Hal opened his mouth to argue, but she quickly said, "I wanted the rest to go for a scholarship in her name."

His mouth shut with a click.

"A scholarship?" Patty wiped a tear from her cheek, her hand shaking.

"Yes. I thought I'd leave the details up to you. I won't be here to organize it."

Patty nodded. "I will be honored to do this. Thank you, Miriam."

She cleared her throat. "Dina was my best friend. I will always miss her."

She left their house ten minutes later. Her eyeballs itched behind the reddened lids. Patty had nearly squeezed all the air from her lungs when Miriam stood to return to her apartment. Both she and Hal wished her well in the future and agreed to do what she wished with the money. It had been a good way to spend it.

Two days later, she sold her car and hired a driver to take her back to Sutter Springs.

"This is it, Ella Mae," she whispered to her daughter. "We're going home. Soon, we'll be back with my sister. Then we'll see Caleb and ask if he still wants us."

It was a rather nerve-wracking thought.

Their first stop was Beth's house. When she showed up, Beth ran out, despite the extra roundness to her shape. The sisters hugged, swaying side by side. Gideon came out and gave her a one-armed hug. Then he picked up Ella Mae. "I'll take her into the *haus*. She can play with her cousin."

Miriam and Beth walked around the farm, arm in arm.

"Gideon's parents moved to the *dawdi-haus*. There's plenty of room for you and Ella Mae to stay with us."

"I don't want to be a burden. It will be a while until the bishop lets me join the church."

Beth sighed. "And then you'll marry Caleb."

"If he still wants me."

"Don't do that. He's a *gut* man. According to Zeke, he's been working overtime. Keeping busy so his mind doesn't dwell. He'll be happy to see you."

"Beth, I'm sorry I wasn't a better sister."

"Well, you weren't easy. Maybe you needed longer to grow up. We have time."

She nodded, her heart full with her sister's forgiveness. Tomorrow, she'd meet with the bishop. Then she'd go see Caleb.

"How long will you work this evening?"

Caleb gave the nail three more solid whacks with his hammer, then set down the tool. He grabbed the damp washcloth sitting on the step stool and wiped his hands, face, and neck, clearing away the dust and sweat.

"I'm almost done," he told Zeke. "Then you and your *daed* and brother can start planning to paint."

Zeke scoffed. "You know we are in no hurry. The family won't move in for another three weeks. We have plenty of time."

"*Ja.* This is true."

A young couple had recently purchased the *haus* from an older *Englisch* couple who planned to move south permanently. According to the *Ordnung*, the couple had a year to make the *haus* fit the guidelines. The electrical had been ripped out in the *haus*, but left in the barn since the man was a dairy farmer. Some of the bishops allowed indoor plumbing, so they hadn't removed it.

Caleb had been brought in to redo all the cabinets and cupboards. The old ones had begun to rot and were spotted with mold and mildew. He could smell the dank odor the first time he'd entered the *haus*.

With the new cabinets installed, the odor had vanished. He was pleased with his work.

"Brother, you know I wasn't referring to the time frame for the project." Zeke settled a hand on his shoulder. Caleb froze. He'd been avoiding this conversation for weeks. Ever since he let Miriam walk away. "You work until almost dark, sometimes through suppertime. You are out and working again right after chores. Molly is worried. So is your *mamm*."

The guilt stabbed him, hard. He hadn't meant to cause his family concern.

But whether it's what he intended or not, the result mattered. He turned to face his brother-in-law.

"I don't know what you expect me to tell you."

"I expect you to tell me why you are avoiding your own family. We are not going to judge you. Only *Gott* can do that. But we are confused why you won't talk to us. Caleb, Molly missed you for three years when you were in a coma. Don't make her lose you again."

Caleb sucked in a breath. Oh, that hurt. Thinking of his sweet sister dealing with his being unconscious and unresponsive for so long. When he'd come back to her, she'd never complained about the length of time he needed for rehab, or all the things he had to relearn. Such as walking.

"She's not going to lose me again!"

Zeke lifted an eyebrow. "You are not considering leaving the community for the *Englisch* world."

Caleb blinked. Even when Miriam had been here, that had never entered his head.

Thinking of her brought a familiar pain to his chest. He rubbed at it, trying to soothe it away.

"*Nee.* I am Amish. This is where *Gott* put me. I won't break my baptism promise." Although, he wondered, if he'd been that absent from his family, did that count as breaking faith with his church?

"Are you in love with her? With Miriam?"

Zeke might have been known as the quietest of the five Bender siblings, but he was also known for being the bluntest. He said what he meant, never dressing it up or trying to be overly polite. Sometimes, it was appreciated. Sometimes, it was disconcerting.

Like now.

Caleb hesitated, uncertain how to respond. In the end, he went with the unvarnished truth. "*Ja*, I love her."

"But she's *Englisch*."

Still, no judgment. Just a clarification. His sister had married a rare fellow.

"For now." Caleb sighed and sat on the step stool. Zeke leaned against the finished countertop. "When she left, Miriam said she needed to get her life in order. She had some financial obligations she needed to attend to. She also wanted to see if Owen McCallister would receive a harsher sentence. She didn't want him to get out and *cumme* here to find her. Again. She wasn't sure how long that would be. When that was done, she said she'd be back."

"You know that our family hasn't always had the best opinion of her?" Zeke scuffed his boot lightly against the floor.

Caleb didn't want to hear about her bad points. In his mind, they'd all been dealt with long before she reentered his life. "I'm aware. She's changed. She's brave. Honest. Lovely in all the ways that matter."

Zeke nodded. "I agree. Beth has been in contact with her and is thrilled to be renewing their relationship."

He swallowed the emotion filling his throat and squeezing his lungs. "She said that was one of the issues. That she needed to know her sister would *welkum* her if she returned."

"Why didn't you tell her you'd wait with her while she waited for his sentencing?"

"Honestly, I never thought of it. If I had, then I would have gone. I wish I had. Then she'd know for sure that I loved her, and would support her, no matter what."

"I already know that."

Both men swung around, their mouths dropping open.

Miriam stood in the doorway, her beautiful hair modestly covered with a crisp *kapp*. She was wearing a jade-green dress with a white apron.

"Miriam," he breathed, barely aware of Zeke excusing himself to allow them to talk alone. "You're back. To stay?"

"Yes." She held up her hand. "I left Ella Mae with your mom and sister and came straight here."

She took a step closer to him. "I want to be clear. I love you. And I want to be with you. But I needed to make sure this was the path God wanted me to take. That's why I stayed away so long. It took a lot of prayer. I knew it would be hard to return to the Amish way of living. But not as hard as I thought it would be."

"When did you return?" He was a little hurt she hadn't *cumme* to him first, but he tried to keep that out of his voice.

"Please don't be upset with me."

He hadn't hidden it well. "I missed you so much. Every day, I wondered if you would return. You were never far from my thoughts."

"I know. It was the same for me."

Her hand reached out and hovered near his cheek, almost as if she feared touching him. He brought his own hand up and cupped hers, bringing them both to cover his heart, letting her feel the strong steady beat pulsing with love for her.

"I had stopped to see Beth before I left here before. She gave me some clothes. I needed to see if I could return, really return, to that life before I lifted your hopes. I went back to Columbus and sold everything of value I had. I gave all the money to Dina's family to pay off the debt from her funeral. They are starting a scholarship fund with what is left over. I prayed. Oh, Caleb, I prayed so hard. The moment I heard Owen arrived at the maximum-security prison and was serving life without the option for parole, I sold my car, hired a driver, and returned. I had to see my sister first. I needed her to come with me to talk to the bishop."

Excitement built like lava bubbling in a volcano. He wouldn't be able to contain it much longer.

"*Ja?* What did the bishop say?"

She grinned. "He said I have to make a public apology in church. Then I have to go through some classes. It might take six months, but if all goes well, in six months, I can be baptized."

With a loud whoop, Caleb picked her up and swung her around.

Miriam laughed and snuggled her face into the curve of his neck. He set her feet on the ground.

When her pink-cheeked face laughed up at him, he could no longer resist. He leaned in and softly touched his lips to hers. She sighed into his mouth. He could smell coffee and mint mingled in her breath.

"I want to marry you. As soon as you are baptized."

"Are you proposing to me? Before I am part of the church?"

"Absolutely. I'm not wasting any more time. I want to marry you and I want to hear Ella Mae growing up calling me *Daed*."

She huffed a gentle laugh that wrapped around his heart. "We can do that. And maybe add a few more chicks to our family?"

More *bopplin*. The things he'd never let himself believe he could have, but *Gott* had opened the door to them.

"I love you, Miriam Troyer. And as soon as I can, I plan to marry you and raise a beautiful family to the Lord."

She smiled mistily.

He caught her lips in a longer, deeper kiss that promised her a lifetime of love and devotion.

EPILOGUE

"Rhoda was a lovely bride," Miriam told her husband of over a year, leaning against his arm. They'd arrived home an hour ago after spending the day with family celebrating Rhoda's wedding to Aaron Lapp. Aaron had been walking out with her for months. When he'd finally asked him to marry her, she nearly said no, believing it was her duty, as the last daughter at home, to care for her mother. Caleb had a talk with her, assuring Rhoda that their mom would always have a home with him, and that Rhoda could marry the man she loved with their blessing.

The Schultz family tended to take their responsibilities way too seriously. Miriam had decided that she would spend five minutes every day focused on making Caleb laugh.

She'd had success with that plan.

They stood on their wraparound porch, enjoying the cool autumn breeze. Miriam sniffed the air gently. The soft fragrance of woodsmoke drifted by her nostrils.

"Someone must have a fire going," Caleb responded absently, his attention on their clasped hands, resting on the railing. "I can't believe my younger sister is a *frau*. Time goes so fast."

Inside the house, Ella Mae giggled. Miriam grinned. "I think our daughter is awake."

He snorted. "I think *Mamm* is enjoying getting her granddaughter worked up."

Sure enough, they heard his *mamm* laughing and murmuring.

Miriam placed her hand on the bump, where her unborn child lay, under her heart. "I wonder if this one will be a son or a daughter?"

Caleb lifted his arm and placed it around his wife, snuggling her close to his side. He kissed her temple. "I don't care. *Gott* will give us whatever kinder He pleases. Every one will be a blessing."

She sighed in pleasure and rubbed her forehead against his lips. Being married to Caleb was a world away from what marriage to her first husband had been like. She never worried about Caleb neglecting her or Ella Mae, nor did she ever doubt his fidelity or love. And, quite possibly the most important difference, Caleb was truly the spiritual leader in their house, the way she believed he was supposed to be. He read to them from the Bible, they prayed together, and he wasn't ashamed to share his faith and how it should be reflected in their daily life.

When her back ached, she shifted her position. Her back had been hurting on and off all day. It was almost as if—

She stilled.

"Miriam?" Caleb asked.

"Caleb, you know how the midwife said the baby would be born in about two weeks?"

"*Ja*. It will go fast, though."

"Very fast. I think she was wrong."

"Wrong?" His hands tightened their grip on her shoulders for an instant then he turned her to face him, his eyes wide in a suddenly pale face. "How wrong?"

"I think this baby wants to be born now." She gasped as

another pain hit, beginning in the middle of her back and spreading around to the front of her abdomen. They would not make it to the hospital in the buggy.

Forcing himself not to panic, Caleb helped his laboring wife inside the *haus*. Once he was certain that she was fine, he ran to the phone in the barn and called to find a driver. He didn't bother with the normal drivers. Finding one who was home and could drop everything to come and assist Miriam this instant was highly improbable. Instead, he called the Sutter Springs Police Department and asked to speak with Molly's brother-in-law, Steve.

"Steve!" he shouted down the line. "Miriam's in labor!"

"Calm down, Caleb. Stay with her. I'll be there soon."

Caleb dropped the phone and ran at full tilt back to the *haus*. *Mamm* had Ella Mae in her booster chair and was preparing her a snack. He skidded to a halt inside the *haus*. He was expected to remove his boots, but he hesitated. The seconds it took to put the boots back on might be important.

"Remove your boots, *sohn*," his mother said, frowning. "Your wife is waiting for you in the next room."

After kicking off the footwear, he strode at high speed to his wife. She walked the perimeter of the room, grimacing, her hands braced on the small of her back.

"Miriam?" He hated seeing her in pain. If only he could take some of it on for her.'

"Don't worry, Caleb. I'll be fine and will be greeting our son or daughter soon. I can't wait to hold him or her in my arms."

She caught her breath again and paused. When she hunched over, Caleb helped her to a chair. "Steve is on the way. He'll bring us to the hospital. My mother will watch Ella Mae for us."

She nodded but appeared unable to speak.

Steve crashed through the door. "Got here as soon as I could. I left Joss with your mom. She'll help take care of Ella Mae. Let's get this show on the road."

Between the two men, Miriam and the suitcase she'd packed the week before were loaded into Steve's cruiser. At Caleb's urging, Steve turned on his siren. The cars parted and let them through.

At the hospital, Steve thumped Caleb on the back. "I'll be here in the waiting room." He sauntered to a chair, sat down, and pulled his phone out of his coat pocket. Caleb followed his wife and forgot about everyone else.

Three hours later, tears streamed down his face when the nurse handed him his *sohn*.

"He's beautiful, isn't he?" Miriam yawned halfway through her statement. She looked exhausted, yet he'd never seen her more lovely.

"He is. So are you." He leaned over and kissed her. "*Denke*, for our *sohn*."

She smiled. "I never realized how much I'd love being a mom. Or a wife. God has been so good to us, hasn't He?"

"*Ja*. He's been wonderful *gut* to us."

Looking over the *boppli*'s head to his wife, his throat closed with emotion. Caleb had never felt more in awe of the wonder of *Gott* before.

"What shall we call him?"

He cleared his throat. He'd thought about this a lot in the past nine months. "Shall we call him Amos, after your father?"

The sun coming through the window caressed her beautiful face. Her smiling lips trembled. "I like that. I like it a lot. I know it's not the normal way things are done…"

"*Ja?* What would you like?" He'd give her the world, if it was in his power.

"I know it's not usual for Amish to have middle names. Although Ella Mae has one, as you know. Could we name him Amos Jude?"

Caleb blinked. Jude, for his *daed.* "*Ja.* We could do that. And if we can't, we can give him a *J* for a middle initial. We'd know what it stood for."

She nodded. Since names tended to be reused within the Amish community, and even in families, *kinder* were sometimes given a middle initial to differentiate those who shared a first name from each other.

She stretched out a hand and laced their fingers together. He leaned over and kissed his wife again. "Miriam Schultz, I love you with every breath in my body."

She smiled at him, her eyes misty. "Ditto."

She met him halfway in a sweet kiss of love and belonging.

* * * * *

Dear Reader,

Sometimes when I write a book, a secondary character appears that demands his or her own story. This was the case with both Caleb and Miriam.

When I introduced Caleb in *Hidden Amish Target*, I had no other plans for him. However, after he awoke from his coma, I wondered what his future would be like, returning home after years with so many changes. I had some readers who wanted to know more, too.

Miriam came along in *Amish Witness to Murder*. I'll admit, I didn't like her that much in that story. At the same time, I wanted to draw her back to the love of God and repair her relationship with her sister.

I hope you enjoyed their story.

I love connecting with readers. You can contact me at www.danarlynn.com. Consider signing up for my newsletter! I'm also on Facebook and Instagram.

Blessings,
Dana R. Lynn

Harlequin® Reader Service

Enjoyed your book?

Try the perfect subscription for Romance readers and get more great books like this delivered right to your door.

See why over 10+ million readers have tried Harlequin Reader Service.

Start with a Free Welcome Collection with free books and a gift—valued over $20.

Choose any series in print or ebook. See website for details and order today:

TryReaderService.com/subscriptions

RSBPA2409